"What do you th...

"Funny." Daniel crossed his arms over his chest. "I was about to ask you the same thing."

"Evie is *my* companion," Blythe said. "It's up to me to decide what she can and cannot do."

"True, but when you seem to focus on the can'ts more than the cans, it's time for me to intervene. What gives? Why aren't you letting Evie do what she wants to do?"

Indignant, Blythe squared her shoulders and lifted her chin. "I'm simply looking out for Evie's best interest."

"Oh, like your parents did with you?"

Blythe took several deep breaths as her cheeks turned pink. "I don't have to take this."

With that, she turned on her heel and marched back down the path toward the camp. She'd had enough of Daniel Stephens and his rose-colored-glasses view of life. Sure, camp was supposed to be an escape, but there was also reality. Kids got sick even when they were having fun.

And she'd do whatever she had to in order to protect them.

It took **Mindy Obenhaus** forty years to figure out what she wanted to do when she grew up. But once God called her to write, she never looked back. She's passionate about touching readers with biblical truths in an entertaining, and sometimes adventurous, manner. Mindy lives in Texas with her husband and kids. When she's not writing, she enjoys cooking and spending time with her grandchildren. Find more at mindyobenhaus.com.

Books by Mindy Obenhaus

Love Inspired

Rocky Mountain Heroes

Their Ranch Reunion
The Deputy's Holiday Family
Her Colorado Cowboy
Reunited in the Rockies
Her Rocky Mountain Hope

The Doctor's Family Reunion
Rescuing the Texan's Heart
A Father's Second Chance
Falling for the Hometown Hero

Visit the Author Profile page at Harlequin.com.

Her Rocky Mountain Hope

Mindy Obenhaus

LOVE INSPIRED
INSPIRATIONAL ROMANCE

LOVE INSPIRED®
INSPIRATIONAL ROMANCE

Recycling programs
for this product may
not exist in your area.

ISBN-13: 978-1-335-48797-1

Her Rocky Mountain Hope

Copyright © 2020 by Melinda Obenhaus

This edition published by arrangement with Harlequin Books S.A.

For questions and comments about the quality of this book,
please contact us at CustomerService@Harlequin.com.

Love Inspired
22 Adelaide St. West, 40th Floor
Toronto, Ontario M5H 4E3, Canada
www.Harlequin.com

Printed in U.S.A.

Trust in the Lord with all thine heart;
and lean not unto thine own understanding.
—*Proverbs* 3:5

For Your glory, Lord.

Acknowledgments

Many thanks to Sheri Peters, Becky Yauger and Allie Pleiter for sharing your stories with me. While your experiences may have been different, you are strong, inspiring women worthy of my utmost respect. Thank you for helping me bring this story to life.

Chapter One

Boy, he needed a haircut.

Daniel Stephens pulled his shaggy blond hair back into a man bun. Not his favorite look, but it would keep the hair out of his eyes.

The early June sun penetrated the thick canopy of pine trees as he knelt, dipping his brush into the red paint. He wiped off the excess on the side of the can before touching up the trim around one of the windows of the cedar chow hall/multipurpose facility. Eighteen months ago, this former scout camp near Ouray, Colorado, had been nothing more than a series of dilapidated buildings. Now, it was ready to house nearly two hundred youth cancer patients over the next two weeks, giving them the freedom to explore and have fun instead of sitting on the sidelines.

"Aw, don't you look cute."

Daniel looked up to see his older brother Andrew heading toward him, wearing a stupid grin.

He stepped onto the chow hall's wooden porch and promptly batted at Daniel's hairdo.

"Unless you care to be doused with red paint, I suggest you knock it off, bro." Job completed, Daniel stood to inspect his handiwork.

"I hope you plan on getting a haircut before those kids arrive. You're looking pretty rough."

"Ah, the kids wouldn't care so much. However, the overseer for the Ridley Foundation might." Daniel swiped his forearm across his brow. "And since she's due tomorrow, a haircut is on my list for this afternoon. Just as soon as the volunteers finish their training." Since this was the camp's inaugural season, he'd requested volunteers get there a few days early so any kinks could be worked out before the campers arrived.

"Well, you know what Mama always said. You only have one—"

"—chance to make a first impression." Daniel rubbed the five-day growth along his jaw. "Which is why I plan to take care of this, too." He wanted everything to be perfect when the overseer arrived. After all, the Ridley Foundation was their biggest donor, covering the majority of the renovations, as well as operating expenses, not to mention all of the campers' fees. So, if he wanted their funding to continue into next year...

He eyed his brother. "Did you get things squared away in The Barn?" Though the barn-style structure was really a miniature hospital, he'd decided the facility should have a fun name that kids wouldn't associate with illness.

"Yep. All of the sliding doors have been installed."

"I'll have to take a look."

"Before or after the haircut?"

"Ha, ha."

Andrew, the second oldest of the five Stephens brothers, grinned. "They look nice. Your decision to go with the stain instead of painting them was a good call. Adds the rustic touch you wanted."

"Good. And since they're sealed, they can be disinfected just like everything else." The Barn was the only new structure at the camp, while the chow hall, staff quarters, camp office and nine cabins, including his, had been renovated. And he owed it all to Andrew. As the former owner of one of the largest commercial building companies in Denver, his brother had all the know-how needed to do the job not only to regulation, but also to finish it under budget and on time.

They scanned the sun-soaked grassy area surrounding the flagpole at the center of the camp while a grosbeak sang sweetly in a nearby tree. Daniel could hardly wait to see campers running to and fro. For many of them, this would be their first time experiencing summer camp. And he was determined to see to it they had the time of their lives—a week full of fun and adventure.

"The place looks great, Daniel." Andrew slapped him on the back. "Mama would be proud of you."

A lump formed in Daniel's throat. As the youngest of five boys, he'd always loved adventure. Mountain climbing, ice climbing, extreme snowboarding, white water rafting… Nothing was off-limits. And his parents had never held him back. Then his mother was diagnosed with cancer.

As she neared the end of her battle, she'd asked to join him on one of his adventures. And while it had only been white water rafting on the nearby Uncompahgre River, the experience got him to thinking about others whose hopes and dreams had been dashed by cancer—kids who didn't get to be kids because of this dreaded disease that forced them to endure things they should never have to go through.

Somehow, God had taken that nugget of an idea and turned it into a reality.

The sound of a vehicle on gravel drew his attention to the camp's main drive as a white Camry emerged from trees.

"You expecting someone?" asked Andrew.

Daniel eyed the vehicle as it wound past the camp office that now doubled as his sleeping quarters. "No, I'm not."

They continued to watch as the driver came to stop next to a towering spruce. A moment later a woman emerged. Her light-brown hair was slicked back into a sleek bun, and she wore skinny jeans topped with a dark blazer over a white shirt. He did a double take then. Why was she wearing *heeled* booties? They might be stylish, but they definitely weren't practical out here.

Yep, this gal was a professional of some sort. And about as out of place as a vegetarian at a barbecue cook-off.

He couldn't tell if she saw him or not, though she seemed to be scanning the area with a critical eye.

He leaned toward Andrew. "Do you think she's lost?"

"Don't know. But I'm sure you'll handle it just fine." Shoving his hands into the pockets of his faded jeans, Andrew strolled off the porch and headed toward his truck. "Have fun."

Daniel wasn't sure about fun, but he was curious. He picked up the paint can and his brush and trekked along the dirt path toward his office, waving as Andrew pulled away. Maybe she was an inspector of some sort.

No, not dressed like that. Besides, inspections had all been signed off on. So, what could she want?

He observed the woman again. Maybe she was from

one of those pharmaceutical companies. Those folks always dressed like they'd come straight from a business meeting, and with the new medical facility...

Unfortunately, the medical staff was tied up with today's training.

"Can I help you?" he asked as he approached.

Her head jerked in his direction, her scrutinizing gaze moving from his greasy hair and scruffy beard to his paint-spattered Wild Child T-shirt, cargo shorts and flip-flops before returning to his face again. "I'm looking for Daniel Stephens."

Confused and perhaps a little embarrassed by his appearance, he said, "I'm Daniel."

Her large eyes widened even more, her pink lips forming a slight O. "*You're* Mr. Stephens?" Her exaggerated blink made it clear she couldn't believe what she was seeing.

Shoving his insecurity aside, he straightened and sent her his best smile. "I am. And you are...?"

She extended her hand, long fingers tipped with perfectly manicured nails. "Blythe McDonald. Overseer for the Ridley Foundation."

His smile evaporated, his confidence and heart sinking somewhere in the vicinity of his knees. "You're...? I wasn't expecting you until tomorrow."

"Today is June eighth, correct?"

"Yes, but your email said June ninth."

"Then you must have read it incorrectly." Her forced grin grated his suddenly frazzled nerves.

Sure, the camp was ready, but he wasn't. He'd seen vagabonds who looked better than he did. And the welcome speech he'd been rehearsing for the past week had flown completely out of his brain. If he didn't find a way to redeem himself soon, he could forget about any funding from the Ridley Foundation, and the camp he'd worked so hard to bring back to life would be a goner.

And the kids…the ones who were looking forward to an escape from the world of cancer. Camp Sneffels was supposed to be a haven for them—a place where they could feel normal and experience things they might otherwise miss out on. Things such as zip-lining, a challenge course, canoeing… Most of all, they'd get to be with other kids who understood what they were going through and, perhaps, realize they weren't so different after all.

They were the ones who would suffer. And he would do anything to prevent that from happening.

Staring at the scruffy camp director, Blythe found herself questioning her boss's judgment. Jack Hendershot had gushed about Daniel Stephens for months, claiming, "He may be young, but he knows what he's doing."

Blythe puffed out a laugh. Not from where she stood, he didn't.

Because while Camp Sneffels appeared to be a beautiful setting, its director looked like a bum. Throw in the fact that he couldn't even remember her arrival date, something that should have been of utmost importance to someone seeking funding, and she found him sorely lacking. If he ran the camp with that same lackadaisical attitude, it was the children who would be let down, the same way she'd been, and there was no way she'd stand for that—even if it meant pulling the camp's funding.

"Let me clean this paintbrush, and I'll give you a tour." Daniel Stephens walked away, the *thwap*, *thwap* of his flip-flops echoing in his wake.

Drawing in a cleansing breath of mountain air, she listened to the breeze whisper through the towering pine trees as she inspected her surroundings. Several yards to her left, a smallish wooden building was labeled Camp Office, while straight ahead on the opposite side of an expansive grassy area stood a large, somewhat charming structure with a rustic stone chimney. To its right was a red-and-white metal building that resembled a barn. And surrounding it all, mountain peaks with just the slightest hint of snow seemed to stand guard. Picturesque indeed.

Turning, she opened her car door and retrieved her phone to take some pictures. But one look at the screen revealed two text messages from her boss.

She read the first one.

Are you there yet?

Jack's excitement reminded her of a little kid.

What do you think about Daniel? He's great, isn't he?

She shook her head. *Great* was not a word she'd even come close to using to describe Mr. Stephens.

Her phone rang then, her sister's name appearing on the screen.

"Hey, Jenna. What's up?"

"Just checking to make sure you made it safely to the camp." Though Jenna was ten years older than Blythe and married with two kids, they were best friends. Her sister was the one she counted on to be there for her, to help her talk through her problems and listen to her vent. Blythe could be real with Jenna, something she'd never been able to do with their mother.

"About five minutes ago."

"And…?"

Leaning against her vehicle, she peered down the wooded trail to her left. "The camp itself appears to be all right. Beautiful setting, but the director leaves a lot to be desired. Would you believe the guy wasn't even expecting me?"

"Why not?"

"He thought I was coming tomorrow. And to make matters worse, he looks like something the cat dragged in."

"Now Blythe, you know you shouldn't judge someone by their outward appearance. It's the heart that matters."

She cupped her free hand around the microphone. "Jenna, not only is he dressed like a bum, *he has a man bun*!" she whispered emphatically.

Her sister chuckled. "He can't be that bad."

"Oh, yeah. I'll send you a picture." Movement out of the corner of her eye captured her attention. "Here he comes. I gotta go." She ended the call and secretly snapped a photo of him walking toward her, hands shoved into the pockets of his baggy shorts while he looked the other way. A couple of screen taps and the image was on its way to Jenna.

"I apologize for the mix-up." He stopped in front of her, appearing rather sheepish. "Can I get you anything? Some water maybe?"

She slipped her phone into her back pocket. "No, thank you."

"Do you need to freshen up?"

Peering up at him, she instinctively smoothed a hand

over her hair. Did she look like she needed freshening? Not that she should care.

She stiffened her spine. "I'm fine, thank you."

"All right then. Since you're going to be here for a while, why don't I just give you a quick overview of the place for now? Then tomorrow we can cover things more in-depth."

"That sounds reasonable." After that five-hour drive, she could stand some downtime. Maybe do a little yoga to stretch her muscles.

He pointed toward the large structure opposite them. "That's the chow hall and multipurpose building over there. It's pretty much the hub of the camp. Aside from meals, it's a general gathering place for events."

"What types of events?" She wanted specifics, not empty promises.

"Skits, sing-alongs, a dance party…whatever we can think of. We'll also use it for games or movies in the event that it rains." He shifted from one flip-flopped foot to the other. "I'd take you inside, but the volunteers are doing some training with our medical staff today.

"If you'll follow me this way." He turned and started down the dirt-covered circle drive, then suddenly stopped. "Are you going to be okay walking in those?" He pointed to her shoes.

Noting his own footwear, she said, "I could ask you the same thing."

His gaze lowered. "Okay then." He moved in the direction of the red building with white trim. "This is the camp medical facility, but we refer to it simply as The Barn." He continued onto the covered, rocking-chair-lined cement porch. "No point in throwing it in the kids' faces that all of them have cancer, even if the building is state-of-the-art and ready to meet any need that could potentially arise, be it urgent or routine."

Having fought her own battle as a teen, Blythe could certainly appreciate that. She was all too familiar with cancer and the stigma of being sick.

"What about the staff?"

"Some of the best in the region." He escorted her inside where she was greeted by brightly colored walls and plenty of rustic wood doors and trim. After giving her a thorough tour of the facility, they moved on to the cabins where he explained that everything in the camp was accessible, including bathrooms.

Returning to where they'd started, Blythe found herself satisfied with the facilities, yet there was still one thing she needed to know. "What sorts of activities do you have for the kids? After all, you did promise them adventure." Just like the camp she'd attended after her lymphoma diagnosis. Yet, instead of fun and games, she and the other campers had spent most of the week either in their cabins or doing nothing more than arts and crafts. Needless to say, she was not about to allow the kids coming to Camp Sneffels to face the same disappointment.

Beneath his bedraggled beard, the corners of Daniel Stephens's mouth lifted, adding a gleam to his blue eyes. "I'll take you to Adventure Haven tomorrow, but we've got zip-lining, a challenge course, fishing, canoeing, horseback riding—"

"And they'll actually get to do all of those things?"

Seemingly confused, he stared down at her. "I sure hope so. I'd hate for the kids to leave disappointed."

His response caught her off guard. Not to mention the sincerity in his tone. Did he really care about the kids having fun or was this simply a ruse?

Chapter Two

Daniel may have been blindsided when he first saw Blythe McDonald, but by the next morning, he was ready for her.

When he tugged open the door to the chow hall, he had his plan all worked out. After breakfast, he'd take her over to Adventure Haven and show her all the outdoor events. He'd get the staff to demonstrate each one, and then she could try them out for herself. Well, if she chose to, anyway. He kind of doubted she would, but he'd at least give her the opportunity.

After that, he'd sit down with her and answer any questions she might have. Of course, how he'd handle the rest of her two-week stay, he had no idea. He hoped she wouldn't be a thorn in his side, annoying him and every other staff member as she observed every detail of the camp.

The aroma of bacon awakened his appetite as he stepped inside the large space where staff and volunteers had gathered for their morning meal. Dressed in his green Camp Sneffels polo shirt along with a pair of khaki shorts, he ran a hand through his short hair as he searched the group. Throw in his clean-shaven face and he was looking and feeling more like a professional. A professional camp director, anyway.

After giving Blythe a tour of the camp yesterday, he'd shown her to the small, private cabin that would have been his had he not needed a place for her to stay. Then he promptly excused himself and hightailed it into Ridgway to the barber. Yet, while he'd given Blythe instructions that dinner was at six, her car was gone when he returned. And by the time she again rolled up the drive, he was too involved in a meeting with his adventure staff to check on her.

However, the fact that he didn't see her here this morning had him wishing he had checked in. Or, at least, introduced her to some of the staff in case she encountered any problems.

She's a big girl. And it's not like you won't be seeing her today.

True. But if she didn't show up for breakfast, he'd be forced to knock on her door. And that was something he really didn't want to do. Blythe McDonald struck him as a woman who appreciated her privacy.

Scanning the chow hall with its old stone fireplace, buckskin-colored walls and wood accents that stretched from the rafters to the wainscoting, he saw his old adventuring-buddy-turned-adventure-director, Levi Chapman, looking all kinds of weird as he drew closer.

"Dude, what happened to you?" His horrified gaze moved from the top of Daniel's head to his hiking shoes and back again. "You look so…official."

"Yeah, maybe you should try it sometime. Might help you find that special woman you keep looking for."

"You got a woman?"

"No." Daniel shot an annoyed look at his friend. "And I'm not looking, either."

Levi peered past him. "Speaking of women, who's that?"

Daniel turned as the door closed behind Blythe. Her light brown hair was again in a tighter-than-tight bun that practically screamed control freak. Was that how she always wore it? Kind of intense, if you asked him. And her bright pink cardigan over a white T-shirt with trendy jeans had her looking like she was ready to hit the mall, not the adventure course.

Leaning toward his friend, he responded, "Someone neither of us would *ever* be interested in."

He watched her for a moment, noticing that she looked kind of lost, tugging her sweater around her midsection as though she was uncomfortable. Her gaze moved past him, then quickly returned as recognition dawned. Why had he not noticed how strikingly beautiful her eyes were? Not brown, not green, not blue. But an interesting blend of each.

Giving himself a shake, he moved toward her. "Good morning."

She lifted her chin. "Good morning."

"I was just about to grab some breakfast," he said. "Care to join me?"

"Thank you."

They continued toward the kitchen at the far end of the room.

"For now, we're keeping things simple," he said. "But once the campers arrive, meals would be served family style, with platters and bowls of food being delivered to the tables."

"That's good." She considered the space. "Avoids

making anyone stand out if they have trouble walking or managing a tray."

"Exactly."

Inside the commercial-style kitchen, Juanita, the camp's cook, waited beside a warming table to serve them. "Good morning, Mr. Daniel."

"Juanita, I'd like you to meet Blythe McDonald. She's going to be visiting with us for a couple of weeks." He groaned inside. Two very long weeks.

"Oh…" Juanita hurriedly wiped her hands before extending one toward Blythe. "I'm so happy to meet you, miss."

Blythe smiled as she shook the woman's hand. "The pleasure is mine, Juanita. And please, call me Blythe."

"Juanita is one of the best cooks on the Western Slope."

The middle-aged Hispanic woman with short black hair and compassionate dark eyes waved a hand through the air. "You flatter, Mr. Daniel."

"No, I tell the truth."

With a wink, she added two extra pieces of bacon to his plate of scrambled eggs and white toast, and handed it to him before addressing Blythe. "What you like, Miss Blythe?"

"Scrambled eggs are fine. Do you have any whole wheat toast?"

"Yes. I'll have it ready in just a minute."

"Perfect." Accepting her plate, Blythe followed him to an empty table. "What a sweet woman."

"Yes, she is." He set his plate on the wooden tabletop. "And her food is amazing. We're blessed to have her."

"How did you find her?" Blythe eased into her chair.

"She was a friend of my mother." He sat, too.

"Was?"

He set his paper napkin over his lap. "My mother passed away four years ago." He met that stunning hazel gaze. "Breast cancer."

"Oh." She looked down at her food. "I'm so sorry."

"Your toast, Miss Blythe." Juanita set the small plate with two slices on the table, saving them from what could have been an awkward moment. All anybody ever said when they learned a loved one had died was "I'm sorry" or "Sorry for your loss." And while he knew it was out of respect, it just felt…weird.

Blythe looked up then. "Thank you, Juanita. Thank you very much." After the woman scurried away, Blythe eyed him, one perfectly arched brow raised in question. "Has she always called you *Mr.* Daniel?"

"No, that's something new. I guess because I'm her boss. She never used to do th—"

"Excuse me, Daniel." Teri, one of the female counselors, or camp companions as he preferred they be called, looked from him to Blythe. "I'm sorry to interrupt, but I thought you should know that Felicia is sick."

"Oh, no. What's wrong?"

"Nausea. Vomiting." Teri glanced at their plates. "Sorry." She wrinkled her nose. "The doctor is with her now."

He looked at Blythe. "I need to go check on her."

"Yes, of course." She set her napkin on the table. "I'll go with you."

Not exactly what he'd had in mind, but he wasn't about to argue.

He burst out the door into the cool morning air and half jogged across the grass, heading in the direction of the cabins, until he noticed Blythe couldn't keep up. Yes, she was speed walking, but her legs were considerably shorter than his. Though those heeled booties weren't helping.

He slowed his steps to match hers.

"What if she's contagious?" Blythe glanced his way as they continued onto the tree-lined path. "We can't risk any of the kids getting sick. What if she has to leave? Do you have backups? Someone you can call on to fill in for her?"

Now he wished he'd kept running. "You sure ask a lot of questions."

"The board needs to know how you intend to handle these sorts of issues."

"Fine, then, I'll let you know *after* I find out what's going on with Felicia."

Blythe didn't respond, and he wasn't about to look at her to see her no doubt annoyed expression.

Fortunately, Felicia was in the nearest cabin.

He knocked, waiting until they were invited to enter. When they did, it was Joel Brandt, the camp doctor, known to everyone as Dr. Joel, who met them.

"Daniel, the good news is she isn't contagious." The doctor looked down at Felicia who was lying on the bottom bunk, her face pale against her dark blue pillow case. "She's pregnant."

The young wife sent Daniel a sorrowful look. "I had no idea. I mean, we're not even trying."

"Based on her symptoms, we did a test." Dr. Joel turned Daniel's way. "The bad news is that this morning sickness is apt to keep her down for a few weeks. I'd recommend you find someone else to fill her position."

"Yes, of course." Daniel smiled at Felicia. "Don't be upset. This is happy news."

"I know." She pouted. "I guess I should call my husband."

"For sure." Daniel stepped forward, reached for her hand and gave it a squeeze. "You concentrate on yourself and that baby, and don't worry about us. We've got you covered." Or they would just as soon as he made some phone calls. Then whoever took her place would have to be brought up to speed and undergo a crash course with the medical staff, but he wasn't about to tell her that. She'd only feel worse.

"Thank you."

With that, he escorted Blythe outside.

As they started up the path in the direction of the chow hall, he could feel Blythe watching him. Wait for it…

"Do you have someone who can take her place?" she finally asked.

"We have a list of alternates, yes." Overhead, wind blew through the trees as he looked down at her. "I'm going to have to make some phone calls, though. So, if you'll excuse me—"

"I can do it."

Call him clueless. "Do what?"

"Serve as counselor in Felicia's stead."

He knew it was wrong to judge, but Blythe didn't strike him as the outdoorsy type. On the contrary, she came across as a city girl through and through.

Clearing his throat, he said, "Actually, I prefer to call them camp companions, not counselors. And each companion is assigned to two campers."

"All right, then, I'm willing to serve as a camp companion."

Blythe as a camp companion. Just the thought made him cringe, making him eager to find a way out of this dilemma.

"Are you allowed to do that? Wouldn't it be a conflict of interest or something?"

"I don't see how. I'm here to make sure Camp Sneffels is worthy of the Ridley Foundation's ongoing support. Serving in this new capacity would only expand my knowledge. I'll simply tell Jack you were short a couns— companion, so I'm stepping in." As if it were that simple.

"Do you realize what that will entail? Campers will be arriving in three days. Everyone else has already completed extensive training. You'll be looking at an intense couple of days just to get caught up."

Her steps slowed, her gaze narrowing on him. "You think I can't handle this?"

While he had no doubt she was smart, how would she manage all of the adventures? After all, there was no spa at the camp.

"I guess we'll find out soon enough." He started to walk away, then thought better of it.

"But you'd better get the okay from Jack first." And if the man happened to nix the idea, then that would be fine with Daniel, too.

Minutes later, Blythe directed a satisfied grin in Daniel's direction. "Great! I'll see you in a few weeks. Thanks." Ending the call, she glanced at the ruggedly handsome camp director standing nearby. Daniel Stephens was definitely not a bum. On the contrary, he looked more like one of those action heroes in the movies. The type that managed to maintain his good looks even when the bad guy was getting the best of him.

Not that Daniel's appearance had anything to do with her decision to step in and take Felicia's place as a camp companion. No, it had been an image of her younger self that did that. The one of the girl who couldn't wait to go to camp, try new things and make new friends. If she'd had a counselor who was as determined to see to it that her charges had fun, then maybe Blythe's camp experience would have turned out differently.

While she couldn't change the past, she could make a difference in another young girl's life.

"We are good to go." Satisfaction filled her as she tucked her phone into the back pocket of her jeans. Serving as a companion would make her privy to *all* of the goings-on here at Camp Sneffels. Meaning it would be tough for Daniel to hide anything from her. Her goal, after all, was to make sure this camp was for the kids and that *they* were having fun. Daniel might clean up well, but he still had to prove himself and the camp worthy of continued funding.

Returning to the chow hall, she and Daniel finished their breakfast in silence. A couple of surreptitious glimpses at the man had her deducing he was lost in thought, though she couldn't help wondering what those thoughts might be. Was he contemplating his next move or whether or not she was cut out to be a companion?

The latter had her steeling herself as they made their way to his office.

"There's some paperwork you're going to need to fill out. I'll also need your driver's license so I can run a background check. And I'll want to introduce you to the staff and volunteers. It's important you know who to go to and for what. Then we'll get you moved over to Felicia's cabin later today. Companions lodge with their campers. Oh, and I still plan to give you a full tour of Adventure Haven."

"Sounds like we've got a busy day."

He held open the screen door to the camp office and waited for her to enter. "Yes, but nothing compared to when the campers get here."

Hmm… He was on point there. If the camp fulfilled its promise, anyway.

The wood-paneled office was small with only a desk, a couple of tall metal file cabinets and four side chairs lined up against the wall to the right of the door. A long, green gingham curtain covered a doorway to her left, making her wonder what was behind it. A separate office, perhaps.

"That reminds me…" Daniel stopped beside the old metal desk and gave her a once-over. "About your clothes."

She looked down at her outfit, self-consciousness tangling with annoyance. "What's wrong with them?"

"Nothing. I'm just not sure how appropriate they are for running around camp with a bunch of kids. We'll provide you with camp T-shirts that all of the volunteers are required to wear, but did you bring any jeans that aren't so…nice? Maybe some shorts, comfortable footwear? Things you don't mind getting dirty."

She wasn't sure she had anything in her wardrobe that she considered play clothes. Either here or at her apartment in Denver. For the most part, business casual was her modus operandi. However, she had brought some workout clothes. Yoga pants and leggings should be all right. And she had a couple of pairs of casual shorts and her running shoes.

She gave herself a mental high five. "Yes, I have suitable clothing, so that won't be an issue."

"Great." He opened one of the desk drawers and

pulled out a small stack of papers held together with a binder clip. "Then once you fill out these forms, you can change, and we'll head over to Adventure Haven." He handed her the documents.

"For a tour." She skimmed the first page, pleased to see it wasn't much more than a job application.

"Yes. And maybe a little fun."

Fun? Looking at Daniel Stephens she had a pretty good idea that his version of fun and hers were miles apart. Still, she wasn't doing this for him; she was doing it for the kids.

A little more than an hour later, she met Daniel back at the camp office, although this time she was wearing a pair of black leggings and a poppy-colored tunic that matched the colorful swoosh on her black running shoes.

"Ready?" He slung a small backpack over one shoulder.

"Yes, sir."

He led her onto a wide path blanketed with pine needles that seemed to muffle their footsteps. Aspen and pine trees stretched to their left and right with little to no undergrowth, and the forest floor was dappled with sunlight.

"How far of a walk is it to Adventure Haven?" Blythe had to take two steps for every one of Daniel's just to keep up with those long legs of his.

"A few hundred yards. Far enough to be separate, but close enough for the kids to manage without wearing themselves out."

She could certainly appreciate that. As would the kids.

"However, I think I'd like to give you an overview first." His steps slowed as the corners of his mouth tipped up into a silly grin.

"What does that mean?"

"You'll see." The glimmer in his eyes did not inspire a lot of confidence.

He led her onto another path that veered to their left and before she knew it, they were climbing. Nothing drastic, just different. The trail became rockier, dust replacing pine needles as they rose above the trees.

The path went straight for a time before making a sharp right turn. Then straight again, followed by a U-turn left.

She wasn't a fan of switchbacks. Or hiking, for that matter. And even though they hadn't gone that far, she found herself huffing and puffing.

"Do you need to take a break?" Daniel called over his shoulder.

"No." She gasped for air. "I'm—" another breath "—fine."

He stopped and faced her. "No, you're not." Lowering his pack, he unzipped it, pulled out a bottle of water and handed it to her. "Sorry, I failed to consider how the altitude might affect you."

"How high are we?" She unscrewed the cap.

"The camp itself sits at just over eighty-five hundred feet."

She almost choked on her water. "A little higher than I'm used to." By more than three thousand feet.

"The good news is, it's not far. Here." He motioned for her to take the lead. "Why don't you go first?"

Why would she do that? She had no idea where they were going. Yet she did it anyway, assuming he would stop her if she was about to lead them off a cliff.

With few trees to provide shade, she began to sweat. How unattractive was that?

Not that she was concerned about being attractive. Except it annoyed her that Daniel was still as cool as a cucumber. He wasn't huffing. Nor puffing. And he definitely wasn't sweating.

At the next turn, she reached to steady herself on a spindly tree. "Ouch."

"Are you all right?" He was at her side in an instant, something she found rather sweet.

"I broke a nail." She stared at her ragged index finger.

"Hmm, that is unfortunate. I have good news, though."

She looked up at him.

"You'll live." He urged her forward.

Annoyed with both him and her fingernail, she forced herself to pick up pace. Dust puffed beneath each footfall. Then she stepped on a rock, losing her footing. She slipped, her whole body tightening as she prepared for impact.

Yet before she hit the ground, Daniel's strong arms caught her. "I gotcha."

Staring up into his mega-blue eyes she swallowed hard. "Yes, you do." She righted herself. "Thank you."

"You're welcome." He glanced left then right. "Stand by. I think I can help." Next thing she knew, he started back *down* the trail.

Where was he going? He'd already helped her, now he was leaving her?

A minute later he returned with a long, rather substantial stick. "Here. Use it as a walking stick. It'll help you keep your balance."

Looking up at the towering adventurer, she simply blinked. The fact that he'd gone out of his way to not only protect her, but to help her, warmed her heart. Perhaps he wasn't such a brute, after all.

"Thanks."

"We're just about there," he said. "But I promise, it'll be worth it."

Strange, but she actually found herself believing him. Quite a feat for someone who was prone to pessimism.

His words kept her going. And only a few minutes later, they came to an outcropping.

"Oh, my." She held a hand to her chest as a view of the entire camp stretched out below her. "It's so beautiful."

"Isn't it, though? From here we can see both Mt. Sneffels—" he pointed to their left "—and the Cimarron mountain range." He moved his hand to the right.

Eyeing the jagged peaks, she said, "This is stunning." She lowered her gaze again to check out the camp. "I can see the cabins and the chow hall. Look—" she pointed "—there's a lake."

"That's where the fishing and canoeing will take place."

"What's that over there?" She homed in on an area just east of the lake, tucked within the trees. There seemed to be a lot of stuff going on, though she couldn't tell exactly what.

"That's the zip line and challenge course."

"In the trees? How is that even possible? And is it safe?"

Daniel laughed. "Safety is our biggest concern here. And yes, everything has been inspected and approved."

He really had thought things through. Too bad she hadn't. Could she really pull off being a camp companion? She wasn't exactly the outdoorsy type. And her black running shoes were now covered in dust. This was so not her.

Lord, how am I going to do this?

Chapter Three

The early afternoon sun was high in the sky as Daniel loaded a cooler full of bottled water onto the golf cart Saturday. He still wasn't sure what to make of Blythe. Or why God had chosen her to meet Daniel's need for a camp companion. Yet that was exactly what had happened. So, whether he understood it or not, he had to trust God's word that all things would work together for good.

After all, it wasn't that he didn't appreciate Blythe's willingness to step up and take on the rigors of being a camp companion. What he wasn't sure of, though, was if she could take it. She was a city girl, after all.

Moving back inside the kitchen, he retrieved the picnic basket Juanita had filled with chips, cookies, granola bars and other snacks before returning to the cart to settle it beside the cooler. While the other female companions embraced the outdoor events, Blythe had been much more standoffish when he'd walked her through Adventure Haven Thursday. As if she was afraid of getting dirty or breaking another fingernail. And that didn't bode well for the kids.

Yet yesterday, when he'd decided to steer clear of any outdoor activities and concentrate on all of the classroom training, she was fully participatory and offered up all sorts of great ideas.

He shook his head. Who knew what today would hold? He and Levi had planned an afternoon of fun for the staff and volunteers with some team building exercises over at Adventure Haven, along with a little free time. If Blythe was half as excited about those as she had been about sharing ideas yesterday, he'd be a happy camp director.

He climbed into the cart and stepped on the gas. Continuing around the circle drive, past the camp office, he spotted Blythe and Teri heading in the direction of Adventure Haven.

Hitting the brakes, he said, "You ladies care for a ride?"

They looked at each other and smiled before hurrying to the cart, which kind of made him feel like he was back in high school.

Wearing gray yoga pants and a green Camp Sneffels T-shirt, Blythe scooted in beside him while Teri sat on the outside. It didn't take him long to catch of whiff of something tropical emanating from Blythe. Her shampoo, maybe? Whatever it was, its sweet scent reminded him of the Amazon Lilies he'd seen on one of his white-water rafting trips in Peru.

Once they were in, he maneuvered the vehicle into the woods, moving up the trail until they reached Adventure Haven where Levi and a couple of his assistants were waiting near the multi-tiered, wooden zip line platform.

Teri, who usually worked as a paralegal at a law office in Durango, leaped out of the cart as soon as it came to a stop and hurried toward Levi while Blythe didn't move.

Hands clasped tightly in her lap, she stared straight ahead. "Teri tells me you're planning to have some team-building exercises out here."

"Yeah, kind of a time for everyone to have a little fun before the campers arrive tomorrow."

She had yet to make any attempt to move. "What kind of exercises?"

"Oh, just some fun challenges, where everyone has to work together. Things like Build a Bridge, Up and Over the Wall, Follow the Leader. Fun stuff."

With the sun filtering through the trees, she continued to watch Teri as Levi harnessed her for a go on the zip line. "I would prefer not to participate."

Twisting to face her, Daniel said, "But you have to. I mean, you are part of the team, aren't you?"

"I'm not comfortable with these sorts of things." She moved to the other side of the seat and stepped out.

With one hand draped over the steering wheel, he continued to watch her. "Come on, Blythe. Everyone else is participating."

Arms crossed over her chest in a defiant matter, she said, "I don't want to."

He studied her, trying to determine if she was fearful or just prissy. Whatever the case, it really chafed him that she would flat-out refuse.

Stepping onto the pine-needle-covered ground, he rounded the vehicle to stand beside her. "I don't know how you expect to encourage the kids to do any of these things when you won't do them yourself. This—" he swept his arm wide, indicating the complex matrix that was the zip line and challenge course "—is why most of them are coming to camp in the first place. They're tired of sitting on the sidelines. They want to experience the game."

"I want them to experience it, too. I want them to have fun and try new things."

He looked down at her, hating that he was now questioning why God had put her in his path. "I see how it is. Do as I say, not as I do."

Her glare darted to him.

"Well, forgive me," he said, "but I'd prefer my camp companions to lead by example."

She walked away as other staff and volunteers began to arrive.

Just as well because he needed to reel in his anger. How could she refuse to participate?

People waved, chatting as they passed him on their way in.

Still waiting for his anger to dissipate, he grabbed the cooler and hauled it to a nearby picnic table, then did the same with the snacks. He couldn't remember the last time he'd been this upset. Even his brothers, who knew all too well how to push his buttons, had never succeeded in making him this mad.

When it appeared everyone had arrived, Levi gathered them to announce how the events would unfold.

Teri came alongside Daniel as he watched his friend. "Where's Blythe?"

He glanced to his right, noticing the outline of her petite figure standing near the lake beside a row of canoes. "Over there." He pointed beyond the edge of the woods.

Teri looked confused. "Is something wrong?"

"Why don't you ask Blythe?"

With a shrug, Teri took off in Blythe's direction.

Daniel immediately felt like a heel. This wasn't Teri's problem to deal with, it was his. Yet here he stood.

Lord, do You really want Blythe to be in this position of camp companion, or did I misunderstand You? After all, just because Jack said she could take on the role, didn't mean God wanted her to.

Levi directed a question his way from the front of the group.

After answering, Daniel glanced toward the lake again. Teri and Blythe were talking, even laughing. Had she explained to Teri why she was over there and not with the group? And why did it bother him so much that they were laughing together?

Focusing on Levi atop one of the platforms, he tried to keep his attention where it needed to be. Yet a short time later, he saw Blythe coming toward him. And for some reason, that made him nervous. What if she decided to quit? Campers would be here in less than twenty-four hours.

She can't quit completely—she's the overseer.

Like that was a positive.

She stopped beside him, but didn't say a word initially. After a moment, though, she leaned toward him, arms crossed. "I'm afraid." Her voice was so low he almost didn't hear her.

"What are you afraid of?"

She shrugged. "Embarrassing myself. Getting hurt..."

"Why would you—?"

She looked up at him then, and the genuine fear in her pretty eyes silenced him. He wondered why he hadn't noticed it before.

"But Teri encouraged me to at least give things a try," she added.

"How?"

Just then, Teri called Blythe's name. And as Blythe turned to walk away, she smiled. "She said please."

When Blythe volunteered to be a camp companion, she'd envisioned herself cheering campers on as they tackled the challenge course or took flight on the zip line. What she hadn't counted on was being an active participant.

Obviously, she should have asked for all of the facts first, *then* made an informed decision. Instead, she'd jumped right in, eager to help the kids, never imagining something like Adventure Haven. The enormity of this place was unlike anything she'd ever seen.

Standing at the edge of the small lake earlier today, she'd wrestled with herself, torn between facing her fears and just giving up. Which, in turn, meant letting the kids down.

Then Teri came along and not only encouraged her, but helped her see that she wasn't the only one who felt that way. Still, what Daniel had planned for her next might be pushing it.

With the team building stuff over and everyone back at camp, he'd been determined to familiarize Blythe with each of the outdoor events, something the other companions had already done. Never mind that her body was already sore from the team exercises. Though, she had to admit, it had been fun. Who knew that trying to get half a dozen people over a wooden wall in the fastest amount of time could be so enjoyable? She'd been the last one to make it, of course. And if her team-mates hadn't pulled her over, she'd still be there.

Perhaps she truly was an arts-and-crafts kind of girl. But that wasn't about to stop Daniel. He'd started his instructional tour at the lake where canoeing proved to be quite a challenge for her and fishing had been a fiasco. If she never had to bait another hook, that would be fine by her.

Now, with the late afternoon sun dancing through the trees, they were at the zip-line tower, and the possibilities of what could go wrong here were too numerous to count.

Atop the wooden platform, she eyed the mountains in the distance. "Did I mention that I'm afraid of heights?"

"Blythe, you can't allow yourself to be a prisoner of your fears." Daniel rummaged through a plastic bin. "Life is an adventure. Besides, you'll be wearing a harness." He held one up before setting it aside and continuing to dig.

"How will that help me if the line itself loosens from the post and comes crashing down?"

He paused his search and gave her a matter-of-fact look. "Blythe, the cables are bolted into the posts. They've been inspected multiple times. They're not coming down."

She knew he was trying to make her feel better, but he wasn't succeeding. "They said the *Titanic* was unsinkable."

Hands on his hips, he blew out an exasperated breath. "Look, Blythe, I truly appreciate you volunteering to be a camp companion. There's a lot to that role, and you've been a real trouper these last few days. But if you're not cut out for this type of work, just tell me."

Studying the intricate web of cables and platforms, she said, "I just don't understand why the camp companions have to do all of these activities."

"They don't, actually." He reached into the box again. "However, I want them to be familiar with every aspect of them."

Indignation stiffened her spine. "You mean the other counselors didn't have to do all of these things?"

"No." Holding a helmet, he faced her once again. "They chose to."

Her shoulders sagged. "Oh. So, what do you do if there's a camper who doesn't want to participate in something?"

"We give them a pep talk, the way Teri did with you. Encourage them to give it a try. But we're not going to *make* them do anything, Blythe." He handed her the helmet. "Here, put this on."

"Why?"

"You need to know how to properly fit a helmet so you can assist the kids with theirs."

"Oh." She put it on.

"Make sure it's seated forward, not on the back of your head." He demonstrated with his own. "Then turn the knob at the back to tighten. It should be fitted, not loose."

Despite her misgivings, she did as he instructed, because the kids' safety was her top priority.

With his own headgear in place, he checked hers. "Good job."

Next, he handed her the strappy looking thing he'd referred to as a harness.

"What am I supposed to do with this?"

"Put it on so you can help the kids. Simply step into

it like pair of pants." He showed her how, and she followed suit. "Then cinch the straps."

She watched him, then adjusted the belt around her hips.

"All right. Now we attach the lanyard by slipping the looped end of it through the anchor point on the front of the harness." He pulled the hook end up while she copied him. "Then, we weight the harness." He clipped his hook to the zip line and reached for hers.

Panic rippled through her. "What are you doing?"

"Teaching you how to weight the harness." He clipped her lanyard to the line. "The staff will hook you to the line, then you'll pretend to sit to put some weight on the harness. That way you can make sure everything is snug."

After an initial hesitation, she did as he said and easily adjusted all of the straps. "Looks like I'll have no problem helping the kids." She looked at him. "Now what?"

"That's it." His grin was suddenly mischievous. "See you on the other side." With that, he pushed off the platform and went sailing through the trees, leaving her sputtering in his wake.

What did he think he was doing? Because if he thought she was going to join him, he was sorely mistaken.

Great. She looked around, wondering what she was supposed to do now. She eyed the clip attached to cable. All she had to do was figure out how to undo that, then she could climb down off the platform. Problem was, Daniel had attached the thing so quickly, she hadn't seen how it was done.

Standing on her tiptoes, she eyed the clip above her

head. "That's nothing more than a carabiner." Not very secure, if you asked her. When she tried to open it, though, it wouldn't budge.

"Problem?" Daniel hollered from the opposite platform some fifty yards away.

"How do I release this?" She motioned toward the carabiner.

"You have to—" A breeze blew through the trees just then, rustling leaves and pine needles and making it impossible to hear what he was saying.

"...twist the release," she heard him say when the wind subsided. Something easier said than done. She couldn't get the thing to turn.

Now she was getting annoyed.

"You could always join me over here," he shouted.

"Or you could come back and help me."

If you're not cut out for this type of work...

Daniel's words played across her mind, tormenting her. He thought she was a wimp.

Okay, so maybe she was used to playing it safe. But it wasn't totally her fault.

Her parents had sheltered her, especially after her cancer diagnosis. And while it had initially bothered Blythe, she'd eventually come around to their way of thinking, choosing to push herself academically. Setting goals and doing whatever it took to attain them. Still, they were safe.

This—she stared at the ground some forty feet beneath her, then the expanse of cable that stretched between her and Daniel—this was way out of her comfort zone.

But it might be fun.

Where had that come from?

She recalled that summer she went to camp. The way she'd pored over the camp's brochure prior to going. There had been one thing she'd wanted to try more than anything. But her dream of zip-lining had never come true.

Again, she stared across the expanse. Imagined flying through the trees. Could she really do it?

Life's an adventure, Daniel had said.

She swallowed hard. She was not a wimp. And camp was about the kids.

She eyed Daniel across the way. She'd show him.

With a deep breath, she closed her eyes and pushed off the platform. Exhilaration and a strange sense of freedom overtook her in those moments. And she had a feeling she'd never be the same again.

Chapter Four

Daniel had waited a long time for this day to arrive. Years of planning, prayers and dreams were about to come to fruition with the arrival of their first campers.

Except in his dreams, it was always warm and sunny. While today was cold and rainy.

Taking another sip of coffee, he watched raindrops pelt the windows of the chow hall. This was insane. The whole region was in the middle of a drought. The county hadn't had any measurable rain all year. Barely any snow the past winter. *Yet today it rains.*

His heart sank. He could imagine the campers' dismay as they slogged across the wet ground to their cabins.

God, I don't understand it, but I know You've got a reason. And though he believed that with his whole heart, he still wished he knew what that reason was.

He turned as the front door opened. To his surprise, Blythe practically bounded inside, looking more relaxed than ever in her green Camp Sneffels rain poncho. She brushed off the hood, revealing a sassy ponytail in the place of the pristine bun she'd worn since the day she arrived. Her smile added a definite sparkle to her extraordinary eyes.

Shaking his head, he puffed out a chuckle. Whatever had transpired on that zip line yesterday had brought out a side of Blythe that seemed to surprise even her. By the time she'd joined him on the second platform, she'd been a different person—one fearless enough that she'd practically demanded they attempt the challenge course before heading back for dinner.

Spotting him now, she made her way across the stained-concrete floor. "When are the kids supposed to be here?"

"Between eleven and two." Downing the last of his coffee, he peered over the rim of his cup to see her gaze narrowing.

"What's wrong?" Her brow puckered. "I thought you'd be bouncing off the walls, eagerly anticipating their arrival."

He lifted a shoulder. "Blame it on the rain."

After a sharp glance toward the window, her eyes cut to him again. "What's that got to do with anything? It's barely more than a drizzle."

"It's enough to keep the kids from participating in all of these cool events waiting for them."

Raindrops glistened off her poncho as she crossed her arms over her chest. "Daniel Stephens, I cannot believe you said that. Where's your faith? It's not like it's going to rain all week. Matter of fact, I checked the weather app on my phone, and this should be out of here in a few hours."

"I know. It's just not the way things were supposed to go. I've been racking my brain, trying to come up with alternative ideas."

"I thought that's what this was for." She swung her

arms wide, sending a spray of droplets to the floor as she indicated the large open space where they stood. "Don't you have some sort of backup plan?"

"Yes, however I don't think watching a movie with a bunch of strangers would be much fun. I've been trying to come up with a game or something that would force the kids to interact with each other."

Her arms fell to her sides. "And thereby get to know one another."

"Exactly."

"Well, why don't we all put our heads together and see what we can come up with."

"We?"

"Yes. You, me and the rest of this motley crew."

He eyed the staff and volunteers scattered about the space. "I hate to ask them to give up what little is left of their free time."

"Are you kidding? These people are invested in this camp. Don't you know that they *want* to help?" Walking away, she headed toward the coffee station where Teri was huddled with several other volunteers who ranged from age nineteen to sixty.

He watched as Blythe chatted with them. Seeing the excitement in their eyes, he suddenly realized that he'd underestimated them. These folks had put their own lives on hold for almost three weeks, given up time with friends and family to devote themselves to those kids who would be joining them later today. How could he possibly leave them out?

Cup still in hand, he crossed to where Blythe was gathered with the other companions, feeling more positive about this little change in plans than he would've imagined.

"All right, let's grab some coffee, pull up a chair

and do a little brainstorming," he heard her say as he approached.

Everyone scattered, some heading for coffee while others made themselves comfortable at a table.

Turning, Blythe almost bumped into Daniel. "Oh, you're here." Her hazel gaze lifted to his.

"I am. And I think this brainstorming session is a stellar idea."

"You do?" Her perfectly arched brows lifted in surprise.

"Yes."

"Oh. Well…" She reached for the creamer as though suddenly trying to busy herself. "The great thing about sharing ideas is that one may come up with something the rest of us would never think of."

"That's an excellent point." He refilled his cup, wishing he'd thought of it, instead of allowing the rain to derail him.

Watching her stir her coffee with a little wooden stick, he hoped his momentary lapse hadn't cost him. Because despite stepping into the role of camp companion, Blythe was still the overseer for the Ridley Foundation. And he was the camp director, the one who was supposed to have everything figured out.

"Shall we?" Touching Blythe's elbow, he urged her toward the group.

While she sat, he remained standing. "I appreciate each and every one of you, not only for volunteering here at Camp Sneffels, but for offering to help us figure out a way to turn what looks to be a rather damp arrival into something that will start these kids' camp experience off with a bang."

"Maybe they could roast marshmallows in the fireplace."

"Good idea." Daniel addressed the college-age fellow. "No camping experience is complete without roasted marshmallows."

"What about some games?" a young woman offered.

"Games are a great idea," he said. "But not just any game, because if you think about it, this could be a great opportunity for the kids to bond. Instead of going their different ways, they'll all be together in here. We need to come up with some games that encourage them to talk and get to know one another."

"Kind of like our team-building exercises yesterday," said Teri.

"Exactly." Blythe scanned the group. "Anyone know of some games that would be good for seven- to twelve-year-olds?"

Since Daniel's internet search hadn't yielded anything, he listened intently, particularly when Cindy, one of their companions, as well as an elementary school teacher, gave her input. He even made notes on his phone, wishing he had consulted someone like her when he was initially planning things. And if he was fortunate enough to have Camp Sneffels continue next year, he definitely would.

Forty-five minutes later, they had an entire afternoon of fun planned. They'd even given it a name. The Camp Sneffels Welcome Roundup. Juanita had agreed to make some special snacks, Levi was off to gather supplies for the games and Daniel found himself grateful to all of them for helping him on such short notice.

"Thank you." He moved alongside Blythe as the group dispersed. "You took the bull by the horns and gathered everyone together. Now we've created the perfect opportunity for the kids to start bonding right away."

"And isn't that what you want?" She peered up at him. "I mean, half the fun of camp is making new friends."

Her energy made him grin. "Sounds like you went to a camp or two back in your day."

Her smile faltered a little. "I went once. And the best thing that came out of it was that I made a really good friend."

"That's cool. Are the two of you still friends?"

Blythe blinked, her expression suddenly vacant. "We will always be friends." She drew in a breath. "Now, if you'll excuse me, I have work to do."

As she turned away, Daniel was pretty sure he saw tears in her eyes.

Blythe had to find a way out of this funk.

Rain continued to trickle from the late-morning sky as she lined up with Daniel, Teri and a handful of volunteers a little more than an hour after their meeting. Shivering beneath her rain poncho, she waited for the first campers to appear.

What was going on with her? First, she'd left her comfort zone by taking a leap of faith on the zip line, then the next thing she knew, she was making a tearful escape from the chow hall. She hadn't cried in years. Of course, she hadn't thought of Miranda in years, either.

Blythe peered up at the towering pines, their needles a vibrant green from the moisture. She and Miranda had been in their early teens when they met at camp and became fast friends. Afterward, they'd chatted daily via phone call or text and, since they didn't live far apart, seen each other almost weekly. Blythe had never had a friend like Miranda, before or since. She'd been the only person Blythe could talk to frankly about life, boys, cancer…and the possibility of dying.

Then Miranda's cancer returned. And within a year,

she was gone, leaving Blythe to navigate the uncertainties of life by herself.

Lowering her gaze, she toed the dampened ground with her sneaker. She still wondered why God took Miranda and not her. Blythe had always been bitter about her cancer, while Miranda accepted hers. Miranda hadn't deserved to die. No kid did. It just wasn't fair.

She drew in a fortifying breath. After Miranda's death, Blythe learned to keep everything inside. Call it self-preservation. All she knew was that if she didn't feel, she wouldn't hurt. And, over the years, she'd become a master. Which made these stupid tears even crazier.

Now, as the first vehicle headed their way, her armor was back in place and she could hardly wait to meet the seven- to twelve-year-olds she'd be spending this week with. She wanted to see these kids having the time of their lives and was beyond grateful to play just a small role in making sure they did.

She eyed Daniel then, recalling the disappointment she'd seen in his blue eyes earlier. Not to mention the spark of joy and excitement as the corporate input evolved into the Welcome Roundup. His passion for this camp and its campers ran deep, and she couldn't help wondering why.

A silver minivan rolled to a stop, pulling her from her thoughts. When the side door slid open, an energetic little boy wearing an oversized Broncos baseball cap on his bald head hopped to the ground.

"Well, hello there." Daniel's blue eyes flickered with excitement as he stepped forward. "Welcome to Camp Sneffels." His smile seemed to grow wider by the moment.

"I'm Micah." The boy thrust out his hand. "And I'm eight."

A tall, slender woman with medium-length brown hair chuckled as she emerged from the front seat to join her son. "He just celebrated his birthday."

"It's nice to meet you, Micah." Daniel shook his hand. "I'm Daniel, and I'm a lot older than you."

While the staff giggled, the boy simply peered up at Daniel with his snaggletoothed grin.

"You don't look very old."

Daniel winked and laid an arm over the boy's fragile shoulders. "Micah, I have a feeling you and I are going to get along just fine." He glanced at the man still in the driver's seat. "You can park over there." He pointed toward the open area to his right. "Then we'll get Justin—" he waved the college student forward "—to show you all to the chow hall so we can get Mr. Micah checked in."

"What about his meds?" Micah's mother's smile faltered momentarily, and Blythe noticed the trepidation in her dark eyes. She could only imagine how nervous the woman must be, entrusting the care of her child, who was in the fight of his life, to strangers for an entire week.

"Yes, you'll take those with you. The medical staff will be there to make sure everything is in order."

The woman's quick nod had Daniel dipping his head to catch her gaze.

"Hey, he'll be fine," Daniel quietly assured her. "By the time you pick him up on Saturday, Micah will have so many memories to share, he might not stop talking for a week."

Blythe was taken aback by his thoughtfulness. This tender side of Daniel was unexpected—not at all like the man who'd argued with her yesterday. Whether she wanted to admit it or not, his sensitivity to this mother's feelings spoke volumes about his character.

"You're probably right about that. He does like to talk." Micah's mother glanced toward her husband and son as the back of the minivan opened to reveal Micah's bedding and luggage. "I've just never been away from him for this long before."

"Tell you what," said Daniel.

Blythe watched as Daniel pulled a business card and a pen from his pants pocket.

"Here's my number." He jotted it on the back of the card. "If you feel as though you can't take it anymore, give me a call and I'll let you know everything he's been doing." He handed the card to Micah's mother.

She accepted it with a relieved smile. "That's very sweet of you. Thank you. Thank you so much."

The woman had taken the words right out of Blythe's mind. It was very sweet of him to do that. Daniel genuinely cared. Something she would have scoffed at only a day or two ago.

Gravel crunched under tires, and Blythe turned as an SUV eased into a parking space. Moments later, another family stepped out, this time with a young girl. Blythe, Teri and Allison, the volunteer coordinator, went to greet them.

"Hello!" they said in unison.

Allison bent toward the girl. "Welcome to Camp Sneffels. I'm Allison, and these—" she gestured toward them "—are my friends Blythe and Teri."

The girl Blythe guessed to be around nine or ten sported post-chemo blond hair and sparkling blue-green eyes. She bashfully looked up at them. "I'm Chloe."

"We're so glad you're here, Chloe." Allison glanced

at her clipboard. "Oh, and how great is this? Blythe is your companion for the week."

As she looked into the child's beautiful eyes, Blythe's heart pounded. Chloe had been entrusted to her for the next week. What if Blythe failed or did something wrong? Even worse, what if she opened her heart?

She looked away. No. She could not—*would* not— allow that to happen. She'd been capable of suppressing her emotions and keeping people at arm's length for years. That wasn't about to change.

Returning her attention to Chloe, she felt something shift inside of her. The angst that had gripped her for the last hour was gone, just like that, replaced by an odd sense of anticipation. Blythe would get to spend the entire week with this beautiful child. Suddenly, she understood why Daniel had been so bummed about the rain. Just the thought of all the fun things she'd get to experience with Chloe sent a wave of excitement racing through her. She was here to make sure Chloe had fun, and that was exactly what Blythe intended to do.

Giving herself a stern shake, she said, "I can hardly wait to get started." Blythe took the girl's suitcase from her father, then slipped an arm around Chloe's shoulders. "We are going to have so much fun this week." She could do this. She would do this. For Miranda, for Chloe and for every other child with cancer who faced a life of uncertainty. She would see to it that this girl had the best week ever.

Chapter Five

The first day of camp was officially in the books. And from where Daniel sat on the front porch of his office/sleeping quarters late Sunday evening, things were looking pretty good. Not only had the rain moved out, today's indoor activities had been a huge success. Thanks in large part to Blythe.

She'd encouraged him to release control and allow others to help, resulting in a Welcome Roundup that was far better than anything he would have thought up on his own. It was a tradition he'd like to see continue. Never had he seen so many happy kids in one place. Campers and volunteers alike had played get-to-know-you games, taken part in a crazy team-building exercise involving Hula-Hoops, and indulged in s'mores and ice cream sundaes.

No doubt about it, Blythe was a creative genius. Daniel was more than impressed with the way she'd embraced not only her role as a camp companion, but the entire camp experience. He sure could use someone with her creativity on his team all the time.

Unfortunately, she'd only taken on the role as camp

companion to help out. He couldn't let himself forget the real reason she was here.

As overseer for the Ridley Foundation, the future of Camp Sneffels rested heavily in her hands. Would she fault him for not having something like the Welcome Roundup already in place?

Taking a sip from his can of ginger ale, he stared out over the darkened, now-quiet camp. And while he knew he should be asleep, too, he had too many thoughts running through his head, making sleep nearly impossible. So rather than tossing and turning, he'd decided to come outside and, hopefully, relax.

With the rain long gone, stars twinkled overhead, while a nearly full moon filtered through the pines, bathing the camp in a white glow. It didn't get much more peaceful than this.

Leaning back in his camp chair, he closed his eyes. He needed to get some rest. Tomorrow was the first full day of camp, and he wanted to be a part of everything. To see the kids' faces as they explored all the adventures Camp Sneffels had to offer. To share in their excitement and ease their trepidation.

The snap of a twig jerked him to attention. Wildlife of all kinds lived in this area. Everything from raccoons to elk to bears... No telling what was out there.

Peering into the shadows, he spotted a lone figure moving along the path. When his eyes finally focused, he said, "Blythe?"

Clad in yoga pants and a bulky sweatshirt, she nearly jumped out of her skin. Fists balled, she said, "Don't *ever* do that again." The words came through gritted teeth.

He bit back a snicker. "Would you rather I send a

Morse code with my flashlight?" He clicked the pocket light on and off.

"Very funny."

He stood from his chair and stepped off the small wooden porch to meet her. "Isn't it kind of late to be out?" It had been after eleven when he crawled out of bed.

Exhaling a breath, she said, "I couldn't sleep."

"Welcome to the club."

She smiled then. "Thought I'd get a cup of hot water from the chow hall and make some chamomile tea." She held up a tea bag.

"Sorry, chow hall's closed."

"Oh." Her shoulders slumped.

"However, I have some cups and a small microwave in my office."

She peered up at him, hopeful. "May I?"

"Sure." He returned to the porch, holding the screen door as she stepped inside.

"What are you doing in your office so late?" Turning, she watched him as he followed.

"This isn't just my office—it's also where I sleep." He continued toward the counter and retrieved a paper cup from the overhead cupboard. "I'll be right back." Shoving aside the curtain that separated his sleeping quarters from his office, he moved to the sink and filled the cup with water before rejoining her.

"No rest for the weary, huh?" Her brow puckered. "How come you don't have your own cabin? Like the one you initially put me up in."

"Well…" Wondering how much he should tell her, he placed the cup inside the microwave and punched a couple of buttons before facing her again. "Actually, that was my cabin."

She looked confused. Then her eyes widened. "Wait, you gave me your cabin?"

"What else what I supposed to do? I didn't think it was right to put you in the staff quarters. You'd have no privacy."

"Oh, and you have privacy here? You work and sleep in the same place."

He lifted his shoulders. "It's not like I'm in here that much. When I am, it's mostly in the evenings, so I don't have far to go to stumble into bed."

There was an air of suspicion about her as she continued to watch him. "Except I'm not in your cabin anymore."

"Like I said, this just makes things easier."

The timer beeped.

She held up a hand. "I'll get it."

"I wanted to thank you for everything you've done," he said as she pulled her cup from the microwave. "Not only for volunteering to be a camp companion, but for helping put together what I think was an amazingly successful Welcome Roundup." He rubbed the back of his neck, which still felt weird with his hair so short. "Honestly, there's no way I could have pulled that off on my own. Thanks for encouraging me to include the others in the planning process."

"Things did work out quite well." She tore open the tea packet and plunged the bag into the hot water. "Although, I should probably be thanking you."

"Why?"

She wrapped her long fingers around the cup and

held on to it like a lifeline. "Because it's been a long time since I've had this much fun."

His brow lifted. "Even the zip-lining?"

She puffed out a laugh. "Especially the zip-lining. Terrifying as it was, I found it very freeing."

"How so?"

She was quiet for a long moment, as though carefully choosing her words. Finally, she leaned her backside against the counter. "I was diagnosed with lymphoma just after my thirteenth birthday."

Her words hit him more strongly than any physical blow and had him taking a step back until he bumped into the desk. "You had cancer?"

"I did." She blew into the steaming liquid. "As a result, my already overprotective parents became even more so." Lowering the cup, she continued. "When that happens, the kids either become huge risk takers or they become like their parents. And, for the most part, that's the route I took."

"The safe one."

She nodded.

"No wonder you were so hesitant when we did the team-building exercises." He shoved a hand through his hair, feeling like the biggest jerk in the world. "And getting up on that zip line platform must have been a major feat for you."

Those amazing eyes homed in on him. "I told you I was afraid of heights."

"Wow." He really was a jerk. Feeling as though he'd lost whatever strength he might have had, he sank into his office chair. "I am so sorry, Blythe." He met her gaze. "As an adventurer to the core, I sometimes forget that not everyone is like me."

"No need for apologies." She started toward him, just close enough to toss her spent tea bag into the wastebasket beside the desk. "Because something happened to me when I was alone on that platform. That young girl who'd once been so trusting and fearless made herself known again. And I can't tell you how good it felt."

"Kind of freeing?"

"Yes. Like it was okay to trust in something or someone besides myself."

"You know, the Bible tells us to put our trust in God, not ourselves."

"Something easier said than done."

"That's where faith comes in." He found himself grinning then. "Who was it who asked me where my faith was earlier today?"

That made her laugh. "It was me."

"Mm-hmm. And look how that turned out."

"All right, point taken." Her slight smile warmed his heart.

"Good. Now, why don't I walk you back to your cabin." He moved toward the door and held it open. "Because if we don't get some sleep soon, we're both going to be hating life tomorrow."

Under a breathtaking blue sky, Blythe held the hands of the two campers who had been entrusted to her care as they moved along the pine-needle-covered path through the woods, headed for Adventure Haven Tuesday afternoon. What a glorious day for an adventure.

Blythe could hardly believe those words had crossed her mind. A week ago, they wouldn't have. But between the awe-inspiring mountain views, serene meadows and idyllic forests of Camp Sneffels, her way of thinking had been transformed. Add in Daniel's little pep talk about trusting in God, and she'd been forced to take a hard look at herself.

She'd gone to sleep Sunday night thinking of Peter in the Bible. How he'd been able to walk on water so long as he kept his eyes on Jesus. When he focused on the storm raging around him, he began to sink.

Blythe had a habit of focusing on life's storms—or the potential thereof. Yet, she was beginning to see just how much more abundant life could be when her eyes were fixed on God.

Again, she took in her surroundings. She couldn't imagine growing up in such a place, yet Daniel had done just that, not far from here, on a ranch outside of the town of Ouray, surrounded by more adventures than she could ever imagine—all of which he'd taken full advantage of, apparently.

It seemed his life had been the antithesis of hers. While she was sheltered, he'd been free to explore just about everything nature had to offer—white water rafting, ice climbing, mountain climbing... Even now, she found it difficult to wrap her brain around such a lifestyle. And that his parents actually let him do all of that.

The man was fearless.

Now, it was her turn to indulge in all of those adventures she'd never had the chance to participate in before. And she was having the time of her life. It was as though she was reliving her one and only summer camp experience. Except this time, she was getting to participate in the fun and adventure that the other camp had failed to deliver.

With the sounds of happy children echoing throughout Adventure Haven, she looked from nine-year-old

Chloe on her right to eight-year-old Evie on her left. Yesterday, their first full day of camp, they had conquered the challenge course and dominated canoeing. This morning they'd rocked horseback riding with Daniel's big brother Noah. Now that rest time was over, it was on to the next adventure.

"Are you girls ready to give the zip line a try?" She peered down at their sweet faces.

"Yes!" Chloe, who wore a pink scarf over her barely there blond hair, didn't even hesitate.

Little Evie, though, had a much more subdued reaction. "I don't know."

"Tell you what." Blythe crouched beside the girl with short golden-brown hair. "Let's just go have a look at it. Maybe that will help you decide."

Pushing her tortoise-shell glasses farther up her nose, she looked from Blythe to Chloe, seemingly pondering the suggestion. After a moment, she said, "We can go look."

The camp had two zip lines. A larger one and a smaller one. Since Chloe and Evie were both on the petite side, Blythe steered them toward the smaller, less intimidating version.

As they approached, they heard the whoops and hollers of other campers as they zoomed through the trees between the platforms.

Still holding their hands, Blythe looked from one girl to the other. "Sounds like everyone's enjoying themselves."

"This is going to be so awesome." The anticipation in Chloe's voice was impossible to miss.

Evie, however, stopped in her tracks as they neared the tower.

Sun peeked through the rustling leaves overhead as Blythe studied the child. Apprehension filled Evie's light brown eyes, which was something Blythe was all too familiar with. Still, she wasn't sure how she should handle this situation.

Then she remembered what Daniel had said when they were up on the platform and she asked him what they did if a child didn't want to participate.

We give them a pep talk. Encourage them to give it a try. But we're not going to make them do anything.

Of all people, Blythe should know how to be sensitive to Evie's fear.

She knelt to the girl's level. "Evie, I know exactly how you're feeling, because until a few days ago, I felt the same way. I went up on that platform, and I was scared."

The girl looked at her, her bottom lip protruding slightly.

"But once I saw someone else do it and how much they enjoyed it, I decided it might be worth giving it a try. And you know what?"

"What?"

"I felt like I was flying. It was *so* much fun. They gave me a harness to wear and a helmet, so I was nice and safe. Now I can't wait to do it again." She paused, allowing a moment for her words to sink in. "So, what do you say?"

Evie shook her head.

Chloe stepped in then. "Why don't we just go up on the platform and look around? That would be okay, wouldn't it, Evie?"

The eight-year-old considered her friend's question for a moment. "I guess so." She took hold of Chloe's extended hand, and the two of them raced up the wooden ramp that led to the platform. They were moving so fast that Blythe practically had to run to keep up with them. Surprising, given Evie's trepidation.

"Good afternoon, ladies." Daniel greeted them on the platform.

Blythe hadn't expected to run into him. "What are you doing here?"

"Just filling in for Ian while he runs an errand."

"Oh." Something about his easy smile and rugged good looks seemed to mess with her mind, stirring up a litany of starry-eyed scenarios. None of which she should be having, about him or anyone else. That wasn't like her.

Add that to the growing list of strange things she'd done since arriving at Camp Sneffels. Her little heart-to-heart with Daniel two nights ago had definitely been unexpected. She didn't make a habit of telling people about her cancer. It was done, over with, a thing of the past. Yet there she'd stood in his office, not only spilling her guts about her cancer but gushing about how being here had changed her. Even if it was true, she wasn't used to opening herself up like that.

"Are you ready for some zip-lining?" he continued.

"We're just checking things out," said Chloe. "See if we think it might be fun, right Evie?"

Blythe smiled at the older girl, appreciating the fact that she didn't belittle her friend, but acknowledged her trepidation as something that was perfectly okay. Which it was, but some kids wouldn't have reacted that way.

"Well, let me explain to you girls how this works." In the shade of an aspen tree, Daniel proceeded to walk the girls through each of the steps, the same way he'd done with Blythe on Saturday.

When he finished, Chloe looked at her friend. "What do you think, Evie?"

The younger girl remained quiet, her gaze lowering.

Blythe could see the disappointment in Chloe's eyes when she looked up at Daniel and said, "Maybe another day."

Evie jerked her head up to face her friend. "You can do it, Chloe."

"No, it won't be as fun without you," she responded.

Blythe's heart practically puddled right there. She exchanged a look with Daniel, knowing they'd just witnessed something pretty special. The selfless act of a friend.

Watching Evie, Blythe could tell she didn't want her friend to be disappointed. Now she was trying to muster the courage to rise to the occasion.

Come on, Evie. You can do it.

After a long moment, Evie squared her shoulders and smiled at her friend. "Let's do this."

"All right, let's get you geared up, then," said Daniel.

While he rigged up Evie, Blythe assisted Chloe. "That was a very nice thing you did. Putting your friend before yourself, understanding that it's okay for her to be nervous."

The sweet little blonde shrugged. "That's what friends do. Good or bad, they look out for each other."

Blythe simply stared at the girl, feeling as though she'd be thrust into the past. Miranda had once said those same words to her. And in that moment, Blythe realized that keeping her heart closed off to this child was a losing battle.

Chapter Six

Despite all of the adventures he'd taken part in all over the globe, Daniel had never been more invigorated than he was right now. From the top of the zip line platform, he watched campers running to and fro, their laughter washing over him like a refreshing waterfall on a hot summer's day. They were having the time of their young lives. Exactly what he'd hoped to achieve when he'd first envisioned this camp. Here, they weren't cancer patients. They were simply kids.

Looking across the expanse to the opposite platform, he saw Chloe and Evie wearing huge smiles as they high-fived each other after their zip line adventure. And there was Blythe, right beside them. She hadn't needed any coaxing this time. Instead, she'd propelled herself off the platform without the slightest hesitation.

"Thanks, boss." Ian, one of his college-age volunteers, moved beside Daniel, ready to resume his duties at the zip line.

"You get everything taken care of?" Daniel removed his safety harness.

"Yes, sir."

"Good deal." He started down the ramp. "We'll see you at dinner."

Approaching the bottom of the ramp, he spotted Blythe and the girls coming his way. Considering that he'd been hoping to spend a couple minutes with Blythe, he was more than grateful Ian had returned when he did.

Since talking with Blythe in his office the other night, Daniel felt as though he had a better understanding of her, yet that didn't keep him from wanting to know more. Especially after watching her on that zip line just now. And the way she interacted with the kids… She not only cared about them, it was important to her that they have fun. Something he appreciated more than she would ever know.

"We meet again," he said as he stepped onto the pine-needle-covered dirt path. He eyed little Evie, recalling her hesitation. "So, what did you think of the zip line?"

"It was *awesome!*"

He couldn't help laughing. "Where're you headed?" His attention returned to Blythe.

"Back to our cabin to clean up for dinner."

"Mind if I walk with you?"

"Of course not."

He fell in alongside her as the girls skipped ahead. "So what adventures have you done today? Aside from the zip-lining, that is."

"Well…" She moved at a leisurely pace. Unhurried, which was fine by him. He was in no rush to get away from her. "We went horseback riding with your brother this morning."

"Oh, yeah? How'd you like it?"

"Are you kidding? With all of this scenery?" She waved an arm through the air. "It was as fun as it was relaxing. And your brother made sure to keep things exciting for the kids, telling them stories and pointing out interesting things."

"Did you know he's a former rodeo champ?"

Her stunning eyes grew wide. "No way."

He couldn't help chuckling. "One of the best there ever was."

"And he lived to tell about it." She shook her head, sending her ponytail swaying. "That's amazing."

"Yeah, he has some pretty interesting stories." He glimpsed the rustling leaves overhead.

"Sounds like you're not the only one in your family who enjoys adventures."

"I never thought about it before, but I guess you're right." His gaze fell to hers. "Though I can safely say that you will never find me riding a bull."

Her laughter reached into his heart, awakening something strange and unfamiliar.

"What does he do now?"

Clearing his throat, Daniel ignored the unwanted sensation. "He opened a rodeo school last fall."

"A rodeo school? I didn't even know there was such a thing."

"Well, there's nobody better to learn from than the best."

Moving from the trail into the main part of the camp, they paused as the girls came to a stop in front of them.

"Aw…look at the cute little bears," he heard Evie say.

He jerked his attention to the child and followed her line of sight. Sure enough, two young cubs were playing just beyond the chow hall. And while they might be cute and generally harmless, where there were little bears, there was usually a mama. And if she felt her babies were being threatened in any way...

"Blythe, take the girls back your cabin. And tell any other companions you see to do the same."

"Okay, but for how long?"

"Until I radio the all-clear. Now, go."

As she scurried away with the girls, he pulled the radio from his hip and brought it to his mouth. "I need all campers and companions to report to their cabins immediately. Companions, take a head count to make sure everyone is accounted for. I repeat, all campers and companions to their cabins *now*."

Slowly, he moved in the direction of the chow hall, never taking his eyes off the cubs even as the voices of kids and companions increased behind him. He thanked God they were doing what they were told.

Nearing the back side of the chow hall, he saw the mama bear circling the dumpster. With the drought, food was probably getting scarce, so they were on the hunt. Lord willing, they'd simply meander back up the mountain. Unless they were desperate.

A moment later, Levi moved alongside him. "They're looking for food."

"Yeah, and we've got a bunch of kids likely leaving crumbs and who knows what else behind." Despite their instructions to dispose of everything properly.

"Bears see that as an open buffet," said Levi.

Minutes ticked by as they continued to wait, and the camp grew eerily silent. If these creatures didn't leave soon, he'd be forced to call the game warden.

Finally, as dinnertime approached, the bears turned to leave.

"Daniel." Allison's voice crackled through the radio on his hip. "We need you in the office immediately."

After instructing Levi to make sure the bears had, indeed, gone, he hurried to his office to find Jacob, one of the male companions, waiting outside.

He moved with determined steps. "This had better be important."

"Micah is missing."

Daniel's gaze narrowed. "What do you mean missing?"

"I thought Zack had him, he thought I had him. But we're both back, and Micah is nowhere to be found."

"You lost a camper?" He couldn't keep the incredulity from his voice.

"How is that possible?" The sound of Blythe's voice had him cringing.

Turning, he saw her storming toward him, anger flashing in her eyes.

"Sorry, I can't answer that right now, Blythe. I have to find Micah." He looked at Jacob. "Where were you when you last saw him?"

"Challenge course."

"All right. You get back to your cabin and don't let anyone leave."

Daniel threw himself into the golf cart parked beside the office. Unfortunately, Blythe hopped into the passenger side before he could get away.

"Shouldn't you be with Chloe and Evie?"

"They're with Teri. You, however, should keep better track of your campers."

He shot her a glance. "That's exactly what I'm trying to do."

He floored the gas pedal, hating that Blythe held

the camp's fate in her hands. This one event could be enough to blow the whole deal.

This was his fault. He should have trained Jacob better. Neither he nor Zack should have assumed that the other had one of their campers, especially in an emergency.

As the cart approached Adventure Haven, he could see that the space was empty—a far cry from what it had been only a short time ago.

He circled the challenge course. Empty. He eyed the zip line. Also empty.

Where are you, Micah?

Canoeing is my favorite thing in the world. Micah had told him just this morning at breakfast.

Making a sharp right turn, he nearly toppled Blythe as he raced toward the lake.

"Where are you going?"

Wishing she wasn't with him, he remained silent for fear he'd say something he'd regret.

"I can't believe this is happening," she ultimately continued. "Don't these people know they're not supposed to let these kids out of their sight out here?"

His blood boiled. He was almost ready to let her have it when he came to the edge of the woods and saw the lone canoe in the middle of the lake.

Releasing the breath he'd been holding, he eased the cart into the meadow and pulled up to the dock. The moment his foot hit the ground, he thanked God for giving Micah the good sense to put on a life jacket.

He made his way to the end of the dock with Blythe right behind him.

Cupping his hands around his mouth, he hollered, "What are you doing out there, dude?"

"I don't know how to paddle." While Micah didn't appear to be scared, he did look perplexed.

"How did you get out there, then?"

The kid simply shrugged.

"Stand by. I'll be there in a sec." Fortunately, the mountain lake wasn't that big.

Daniel climbed into the nearest canoe.

"Don't you need a life vest?" Arms crossed, Blythe watched him from the dock.

Again, he didn't bother to answer. He simply maneuvered the canoe away from the dock and toward Micah.

The still water rippled beneath his paddle and within minutes he was beside the kid. "You know you're not supposed to be out here alone, right?"

The kid lowered his head. "But I was having so much fun."

"I understand, but there's a reason we have rules." He gripped the side of Micah's canoe. "To keep you safe, for starters."

"I put on my life vest." Micah tucked his thumbs in the armholes to proudly show Daniel.

"And I'm glad you did. That doesn't make coming out here alone okay, though. Nobody knew where you were."

Micah frowned. "That's cuz I snuck away from Zack and Jacob." Water lapped at the sides of the canoes as Daniel waited for him to continue. "They told us we had to go back to our cabins, but I didn't want to go."

"Did you ever stop to think there might be a reason we were making everyone go back?"

He shook his ball-cap-covered bald head.

"Micah, there was emergency back at the camp, and

we needed to make sure everyone was safe. That's why you were told to go to your cabin."

The boy's wide eyes jerked to Daniel. "What kind of emergency?"

Daniel hesitated, but the bears were probably long gone by now. "We spotted some bears in the camp."

The kid straightened. "Bears? Cool."

"No, it wasn't cool. Bears can be very dangerous."

Micah's smile faltered again. "I guess I'm in big trouble, huh? Are you gonna call my parents? Am I going to have to leave camp?"

Funny, Daniel wanted to ask Blythe similar questions. Would this cost him any future funding? Would she give him a bad report? Would she be on the phone with Jack before they ever made it back to camp?

"Your parents will be informed, yes. But no, you shouldn't have to leave camp."

The boy's face brightened.

"However, we will be discussing an appropriate punishment for your behavior."

"Oh." The boy's shoulders slumped.

"You will likely lose some activity time and have to do some work instead. Right now, though, we need to get you back to shore." He reached for the line at the front of Micah's boat and tied it to the back of his. "Now you just sit tight and leave the paddling to me."

Blythe was an idiot. Unfortunately, it wasn't until Daniel was out on the lake with Micah that she realized how stupidly she'd been behaving. She felt horrible for coming down on him so hard. She wasn't able to face Daniel when he and Micah returned to the shore. Instead, she silently took a seat on the rear-facing bench of the cart, out of Daniel's line of sight, then hopped off as soon as they returned to the camp and hurried back to her cabin.

Even during this evening's scavenger hunt, embarrassment had her making sure she was nowhere near Daniel. Yet now, as she lay in her bunk, staring at the ceiling while Chloe, Evie and the other ten girls were sound asleep in the adjoining rooms, she knew she had to talk to him. To apologize for her wretched behavior. Because if she didn't, she'd never get any sleep.

Glancing toward the opposite bunk, she saw Teri staring at her phone. So, after hauling herself out of bed, Blythe exchanged her sleep shorts for some yoga pants and asked her friend to monitor the girls while she stepped out for some fresh air. "I've got my phone, if you need me."

Outside, the night air was cool, making her wish she'd at least grabbed a sweater. Goose bumps erupted on her bare arms, but her T-shirt would have to do because there was no turning back now.

Hugging her arms to her chest for warmth, she moved as quickly as possible in the direction of the office, pleased when she saw the light was still on. But a sudden case of nerves had her stopping in her tracks. Daniel truly cared about each of the kids at camp. He would never do anything to endanger them. Hadn't she seen how emphatic he was about her taking the girls to the cabin after spotting those bears?

And yet she'd blown up at him like Hurricane Blythe. All because she'd come in here with a chip on her shoulder, believing Daniel was trying to take advantage of the Ridley Foundation, when nothing could be farther from the truth. He wasn't anything at all like those people who'd run the camp she'd attended. Yet she'd assumed the worst. Even after she knew better.

Now it was time to correct that mistake.

Continuing to the office, she quietly eased onto the porch. Through the screen door, she could see Daniel hunched over the desk, writing something. She'd probably startle him if she knocked.

Not as badly as it would if he looked up and saw you staring at him.

With a bolstering breath, she rapped her knuckles against the door.

Daniel's head shot up instantly, and he looked straight at her. "Blythe?" Pushing away from the desk, he stood and started toward her. "Let me guess." He pushed the door open "You're in need of some tea."

Still hugging herself tightly, she moved inside. "No." Her teeth chattered uncontrollably. "I need to talk to you."

"Couldn't it have waited until morning? You're freezing." Closing the door, he retrieved a jacket from a hook on the wall. "Here." He held it up behind her. "Put this on."

She shoved her arms into the sleeves, grateful for the warmth. "Thank you." The fragrance of fresh air and masculinity enveloped her, and she couldn't help wondering if this was what it would feel like to be held in the arms of man like Daniel.

"What did you want to talk to me about?"

Shoving her crazy notions aside, she looked up to find his uber-blue eyes fixed on her. "I owe you an apology." At least her teeth no longer chattered.

He crossed his arms over his chest then, his bulging

biceps straining the sleeves of his T-shirt. "Go ahead." If he was trying to intimidate her, it was working.

But she hadn't trekked through the chilly night air to stop short of her mission. "I gave you quite a tongue-lashing earlier when I heard Micah was missing. One you didn't deserve. I've seen you with these kids. I know how much you care about them."

"Yes, I do. However, that was a pretty scary situation." His brows lifted ever so slightly. "I am curious why you reacted so strongly."

She could chalk it up to fear or tell him the truth. And while she had, indeed, been afraid for Micah, Daniel deserved the truth.

Tugging the jacket tighter, she said, "Remember when I told you that I had gone to camp once?"

"Yeah, you said you'd made a good friend."

"Yes. Her name was Miranda." Blythe swallowed the lump that tried to form in her throat. "We met at a cancer camp that had promised us fun and adventure, except the directors failed to deliver on that promise."

He lowered his arms then, appearing confused. "You mean you didn't have fun at camp?"

"Other than my time with Miranda, no."

"Was it because of the whole fear thing?" His probing gaze remained fixed on her.

"Actually, I had been looking forward to doing all of those fun things they'd promised us kids. Including the zip line."

"So, what happened?"

Needing to put some space between them, she turned and moved toward the counter that held the microwave. "Basically, the people who ran that camp didn't care about anything but the money. Our counselors were nothing more than glorified babysitters, so we spent most of the time in our cabins."

"Disappointing all of you kids?" He sounded as shocked as he was irritated.

She nodded. "The experience left me rather jaded. I came to Camp Sneffels expecting you to fail. Instead, you've not only exceeded my expectations, you've blown them out of the water. What you're doing here is…pretty amazing."

"Now I get why you kept challenging me that day you arrived, wanting to know about the activities."

She lifted a shoulder. "Camp has to be about the kids."

"I couldn't agree more."

"I know you do. Which is why I wanted to apologize. And, going forward, I promise to judge you and the camp based on your merits, not someone else's failures."

The corners of his mouth tilted upward a notch. "I appreciate that."

An awkward silence fell between them then, and she was about to head for the door when she realized she'd never asked about Micah. "So, what was the story with Micah?"

"He purposely snuck away from his companion because he didn't want to go back to his cabin."

Recalling all the time she'd had to spend in her cabin at camp, she said, "Can't say as I blame him."

"I made sure he understood the severity of his actions, and I called his parents."

"What did they have to say?"

"They were pretty cool about everything. His mom said it sounded like something Micah would do and apologized for not warning me."

"Do you plan to punish him?"

He leaned against the desk. "That's a tough one because I really can't blame the kid for wanting to have fun. Still, he did put himself in danger and caused trouble here at the camp, so I know I'll have to do something, like take away a day of activities, but it's what to have him do instead that has me stumped." He looked at her. "Any suggestions?"

"What if you gave him a chore around the camp? Nothing rigorous, of course."

"I could have him pick up trash. That would still keep him outdoors."

"What if he helped you with something? I mean, you have a good rapport with him, and he'll need supervision."

"Good point. Maybe he should have to be my right-hand man for the day. Whatever I have to do, he's right there with me. And I'd try to find jobs for him to do along the way."

"I think that sounds like a good plan."

Her phone vibrated in her pocket. Pulling it out, she saw a text from Teri.

Chloe is asking for you.

"I need to go." She tucked the phone back into her pocket.

"Is there a problem?"

"I don't think so. Teri just said Chloe was asking for me." On her way to the door, she started to shrug out of his jacket, but he stopped her with a hand to her shoulder.

"Keep it. I can get it tomorrow."

"Thanks."

She hurried back to the cabin to find Chloe in her bunk.

"What's the matter?" Blythe sat on the edge of the bed and smoothed a hand along the girl's sweet face.

"I don't feel good."

"Is it your tummy?" Maybe she'd had one too many treats after the scavenger hunt.

Chloe shook her head.

"What is it then?"

"I don't know." She tugged her mermaid sleeping bag around her chin.

Hmm… The lack of a specific issue had Blythe wondering if it was just a case of homesickness. After all, they were almost at the halfway point, which was when kids tended to start missing their parents.

"Well, how about I stay right here while you sleep, then?"

"Would you?" Chloe's blue-green eyes implored her to say yes.

"I sure will, sweet girl." Still wearing Daniel's jacket, Blythe huddled beside Chloe's bed, deciding she would go back to her own bunk once Chloe fell asleep.

With the comforting aroma of Daniel's jacket swirling around her, Blythe felt her eyes grow heavy. And when she awakened at sunrise, she was still with Chloe.

Sitting up, she eyed the still-sleeping child she'd tried her best to comfort.

Chloe's cheeks were flushed.

Gently placing the back of her hand against the girl's face, a sense of dread wound through Blythe. Chloe was burning up.

Blythe gave her a gentle shake and whispered in her

ear. "Chloe?" She had to find out what was going on. Was it her stomach, the flu or something else?

Yet despite her attempts to wake the girl, Chloe didn't rouse.

Blythe shook her again. "Chloe?" Her voice came louder.

Still nothing.

Teri hurried into the room. "What's going on?"

Blythe met her concerned gaze. "Get Dr. Joel. Something's wrong with Chloe."

Chapter Seven

Daniel had planned for just about any scenario at
Camp Sneffels, including a sick child. But as was the
case with most what-ifs, he prayed they'd never have
to put a plan into action.

That wasn't the case today.

When Teri rushed into his office, telling him Chloe
was sick, the director in him had taken over—assess
the situation, find out what was wrong and then go from
there. But when he arrived at Chloe's cabin and saw how
lethargic she was, his take-charge attitude escaped him.

Dr. Joel immediately transferred her from her cabin
to The Barn where he could evaluate her and run tests,
while not having to worry about the other children being
exposed to any potential illness.

Daniel had called Chloe's parents to inform them of
the situation and, after her fever spiked an hour later and
there was still no indication as to what was causing it,
the decision was made for them to come and pick her up.

Now he waited in a treatment room at The Barn with
Blythe and the medical staff for the family to arrive.
Fortunately, they lived near Grand Junction, which was

only about ninety minutes away. Still, knowing that their child was sick would make the relatively short drive seem excruciatingly long.

He stood at the foot of Chloe's hospital bed, the click and hum of her IV pump echoing around him. Because of her fever, the brightly colored blanket that normally adorned the bed had been cast aside, making Daniel glad he'd opted for the woodland-themed sheets instead of plain white.

He watched the girl drift in and out of sleep, knowing he should go check on the other campers, yet he couldn't bring himself to break away. As though he needed to be assured Chloe was being properly cared for. Not that he had any doubt. Dr. Joel was one of the best cancer doctors in the nation. Still, Daniel felt so helpless. The same way he had when he'd watched his mother slip from this world.

The memory had him stiffening his spine. How could he think like that? Chloe was going to be fine. She probably just had a virus. She'd battle her way back. After all, it was just yesterday she was flying through the air on the zip line.

Blythe remained beside the girl, where she'd been since last night, according to Teri. She held Chloe's hand, wiped her face with a cool cloth, anything to make Chloe more comfortable. Though he suspected the actions were just as much for Blythe, something to keep her busy.

He was glad he'd asked Teri to take Evie temporarily. Blythe wouldn't have been able to focus on her, not when her heart was with Chloe.

When the doctor and nurses approached Chloe's bed again, Blythe stepped back. But instead of merely mov-

ing out of the way as she'd done all morning, she retreated to the hall. And when several minutes passed
and she hadn't returned, Daniel went to check on her.

Sliding the wooden barn door aside, he moved into
the hallway, closing it behind him. He looked left then
right, before starting down the corridor. Swift steps
propelled him across the stained-concrete floor. Where
could she have gone?

He glanced into the small lounge area as he passed,
coming to an abrupt halt. There, in an overstuffed chair,
knees hugged to her chest, Blythe was staring out the
window.

He moved to join her, then hesitated. What if she
wanted to be alone? However, he knew from experience that, sometimes, being left with your own thoughts
wasn't always a good thing. Given the intensity of the
morning and the fact that Blythe had developed a special bond with Chloe, he decided to move in.

Clearing his throat as he entered the space, he kept
his gaze riveted to Blythe. She was still wearing his
jacket and, as he approached, he saw her swipe her face
with its sleeves. Red-rimmed eyes confirmed his sus-
picions. She'd been crying.

He eased onto the arm of the chair. "You all right?"

"Yes." She lowered her legs. "I, uh, just needed a
little break." Her brow was pinched with worry.

"I understand." He glanced toward the window to
see campers moving about. "If you'd like to step outside for a while—"

"No." She promptly stood. "I need to get back to
Chloe."

"She's in good hands." Still assessing her, he offered
a weak smile. "Dr. Joel is tops in his field."

"I know. But Chloe is my responsibility."

"She's all of our responsibility. Each of these kids are."

"Yes, but I'm her companion." Blythe's voice cracked. "Her parents entrusted her to my care. Now she's sick."

Standing, he eyed her curiously. "You're not blaming yourself for that, are you?"

She lifted a shoulder. "If I had paid closer attention, been there for her instead of running off to ease my conscience…."

"Blythe, you weren't gone that long. Chloe was asleep when you left. Even if you were there, you probably would have been asleep, too."

"But why did it take me until this morning to realize how sick she was? She said last night that she didn't feel well, and I chalked it up to homesickness."

"Because she didn't show any symptoms." Fortunately, Teri had told him the whole story.

Refusing to meet his gaze, Blythe shook her head. "I need to get back to Chloe."

He followed Blythe, pleased to see Chloe awake and sitting up when they reentered the treatment room. Her IV was gone.

"Look at you," Blythe said as they approached the girl. "Did you have a nice nap?"

A smiling Chloe nodded, but both Blythe and Daniel deferred to Dr. Joel who was standing on the opposite side of the bed.

"Her fever has finally come down some." The man with a shaved head and warm brown eyes looked at Daniel. "When do you expect her parents?"

Daniel checked his watch. "Anytime."

"In that case—" the doctor turned his attention to Blythe "—if you'd like to help her get dressed."

"Of course." Blythe looked almost relieved to have something to do.

"What about her things?" One of the nurses pulled the privacy curtain around Chloe's bed.

"Already out front." Daniel poked a thumb over his shoulder. "Matter of fact, I think I'll head on out there to watch for Chloe's parents."

He moved into the hall and toward the front doors, his heart wrenching. He hated to see Chloe go, especially under these circumstances. He prayed with his whole heart that it was nothing serious, but he knew that nothing was out of the realm of possibility with cancer patients.

A white SUV pulled up in front of The Barn as he reached the entrance. He continued outside to greet Mr. and Mrs. Whitaker. Concern etched the faces of the couple in their mid-thirties, and Daniel hated that he'd had to do this to them.

"Mr. and Mrs. Whitaker." He extended his hand.

"John," said Chloe's father with a firm shake.

"Amanda." The woman nodded. Her teary eyes tugged at Daniel's heart.

The Barn's door opened then, and Dr. Joel joined them. He introduced himself and said, "I'm sorry we had to bring you up here, but I'm afraid I haven't been able to determine what's causing Chloe's fever. I would suggest that you contact her oncologist and try to get her in right away." He held out a file folder. "Test results and my notes are in here, along with my cell number. If they have any questions, don't hesitate to call."

"Thank you." Chloe's father accepted the folder. "We appreciate all you've done."

The door opened again, one of the nurses holding it while Blythe pushed Chloe out in a wheelchair. The girl's coloring looked better in the natural light, though she was still pale.

"Hi, baby." Amanda hurried toward her daughter and gave her a hug. Releasing her, she cupped the girl's cheek. "How are you feeling?"

Chloe smiled and shrugged, reminding Daniel of when his mother had had to pick him up at school once when he was sick. In front of the nurse, he'd been brave, but as soon as he and his mom were in the car, he'd cried like a baby.

Amanda straightened. "You're Blythe, right?"

"Yes, ma'am."

"I'm glad you're here. I wanted to thank you for taking such good care of Chloe. Daniel told me you stayed with her all night. That you never left her side."

Blythe smoothed a hand over Chloe's spiky blond hair. "I wouldn't have had it any other way. You've got a very special daughter here."

"I think so, too." Amanda reached for Blythe then, wrapping her in a hug.

"I guess we'd better get back on the road." Chloe's father took her bags from the nurse and started toward the back of the vehicle.

As Chloe stood, she reached for Blythe's hand. "I had the best companion ever." She smiled up at Blythe, a spark returning to her blue-green eyes. "Tell Evie to do a zip line for me."

Blythe puffed out a laugh as they inched toward the vehicle. "I will do that."

The Whitakers pulled away as the medical staff retreated to The Barn, leaving Blythe and Daniel alone.

She drew in a deep breath as he checked his watch.

"Shall we go to the chow hall and grab some lunch?"

"You can, if you like," she said. "I've got a date with Evie."

"Don't you think you should eat first? Take a little breather? You've had a rough morning."

She looked at him then, her expression devoid of any emotion. Almost as though she'd willed herself not to feel. "Things like this happen. It's just a part of life with cancer." She shrugged out of his jacket and handed it to him. "Thank you for letting me borrow this. Now I need to go find Evie."

Daniel watched her as she walked away. Something had changed since they talked in the lounge. It was like she'd flipped a switch, turning off her emotions. That was never a good thing because some way, somehow, those feelings eventually came out, sneaking up on you when you least expected it.

And he found himself longing to be there for her when those feelings decided to resurface.

She could do this. Just two more days before this round of camp was over.

By the time Blythe caught up with Evie at their cabin shortly after lunch, she was in control of her emotions. She hadn't even shed a tear when Chloe said goodbye. Now all she had to do was finish out this week, move back to her private cabin and focus on her role as overseer for the remaining week. No fuss, no muss, no emotional attachments.

Hands on her hips, Blythe smiled at the young girl

sporting tortoiseshell glasses and a bright pink head-band. "Looks like it's just you and me now, Evie."

The child's denim-covered legs dangled from the top bunk while her brow puckered. "Where's Chloe?"

"Her parents picked her up a little while ago."

Evie's countenance fell. "But… I didn't get to say goodbye."

The words had Blythe cringing and feeling like the worst person in the world. Why hadn't she thought of that? Chloe and Evie had grown close in their few days together. They'd supported each other. Of course Evie would want to tell her friend goodbye.

"I'm sorry, sweetie." She laid what she hoped was a comforting hand atop the girl's knee. "We couldn't risk you getting sick, though."

Concern filled Evie's light brown eyes. "Is Chloe going to be okay?"

Blythe knew better than to make promises she couldn't keep. Still, she was going to remain confident it was nothing more than a virus. "Eventually. She just needs to be where her parents can take care of her."

Evie was quiet for a moment, then said, "My mom always sits with me when I'm sick."

"And does that make you feel better?"

Her smile returned. "Yes."

Blythe helped her down from her bunk. "So, what shall we do first?"

"We could go horseback riding."

Suddenly, Blythe found herself hesitating. All morning, as she watched Chloe, she'd been replaying the week in her mind. All of their activities. And she couldn't help wondering if, perhaps, the horses had something to do with Chloe's sudden illness. Animals sometimes carried diseases, after all. "Didn't Teri take you riding this morning?"

"Yes, but I love it so much." A grinning Evie clasped her hands under her chin.

"I know you do, but we should probably give some of the other kids a chance to ride. Maybe another day."

"Okay."

Blythe couldn't miss the reluctance in Evie's tone. "Tell you what, why don't we take a walk over to Adventure Haven, and we can decide there?"

Evie's little frown flipped upside down. "Okay!"

In no time, they were chatting up a storm as they skipped along the path to Adventure Haven under a cloudless blue sky. Evie seemed to be a lot more talkative. Then again, maybe it was just that she'd been doing all her talking with Chloe before.

They'd almost reached the end of the path when Daniel came jogging up behind them.

"Hello, ladies." He was barely even winded.

"Hi." Evie waved.

"You doing all right?" He looked from Evie to Blythe.

"Yes, we're just trying to decide what Evie might like to do next."

He looked to the girl. "Hard to decide, isn't it?"

"I wanted to go horseback riding, but Blythe said I should let someone else have a turn since I went this morning."

His gaze moved from Blythe to Evie. "Yeah, that's probably a good idea. But you could go fishing."

Thoughts of sharp fishing hooks and spiny fish popped into Blythe's head. "I…don't think that's such a good idea."

"Why not?" Daniel glared at her.

"Well, it's… Evie probably wants to do something more exciting than that." She shifted her focus to the girl. "Don't you?"

"We could do the challenge course." The child bobbed up and down with excitement.

Blythe peered across the way. "There's an awful long line."

"What about the zip line?" Daniel pointed. "There's no line there, and Chloe even said—"

"I think Evie and I can figure this out." Blythe knew it was rude to cut Daniel off like that, but she had to think of Evie. She had to make sure she made it through the rest of the week healthy.

"What's going on?"

They all looked up as Teri approached with her two companions.

"I'm trying to decide what I want to do next," said Evie.

"We're going to the challenge course," said Whitney, a bubbly ten-year-old. "Want to come with us, Evie?"

Squinting against the sun, Evie met Blythe's gaze. "Can I?"

"Oh, I—"

"Sure you can," said Daniel.

Blythe whipped her head toward him as the girls and Teri walked away. "What do you think you're doing?"

"Funny." He crossed his arms over his chest, his expression intense. "I was about to ask you the same thing."

"Evie is *my* companion. It's up to me to decide what she can and cannot do."

"True, but when you seem to focus on the cannots more than the cans, it's time for me to intervene."

"What are you talking about?"

"Did you even check to see if she could ride horses a second time? And just because fishing may not be your cup of tea doesn't mean Evie wouldn't enjoy it. After all, the point of camp is for the kids to have fun and do what *they* want to do. Oh, and what about Chloe? She specifically said she wanted Evie to do a zip line for her. So, what gives? Why aren't you allowing Evie to do what she wants to do?"

Indignant, Blythe squared her shoulders and lifted her chin. "I'm simply looking out for Evie's best interest."

"As I recall, you weren't real crazy about it when your parents did that with you."

Air rushed in and out of Blythe's nose, her chest rising and falling with each annoyed breath. "I don't have to take this." With that, she turned on her heel and marched back down the path toward the camp. She'd had enough of Daniel Stephens and his rose-colored-glasses view of life. Sure camp was supposed to be an escape, but there was also reality. Kids got sick even when they were having fun. And she'd do whatever she had to in order to protect them.

"Blythe!"

She heard Daniel's voice behind her as she approached the camp. The sound of each muffled footfall as he grew closer.

Still, she refused to acknowledge him, even as he moved beside her.

"I'd like to see you in my office."

Her gaze narrowed on him.

"Now." He turned and started toward the small building where they'd shared far too many revealing late-night chats. Except it was usually Blythe who was revealing some deep, dark secret. Well, not today.

She followed him onto the porch before storming inside while he held the door. Then jumped when it smacked shut behind him.

She watched as he moved around to the other side of the desk. The lines of his face were rigid. More intense than she'd ever seen them. Let him be mad. She wasn't exactly in the best of moods herself.

"All right, Blythe, what's going on?"

"What's going on is that I'm supposed to be Evie's companion and you're trying to insert yourself into that equation."

"First of all, I am the director of this camp. If I think a child's needs or wishes are not being met, then it is my duty to step in. Second, I want to know what's going on with you. All week long you've been having fun with Chloe and Evie, doing whatever it was that they wanted to do. Now that it's just Evie, you're trying to talk her out of everything. I'm surprised you haven't confined her to the cabin for some arts and crafts."

Blythe's gaze shot to his, her heart racing. "How dare you?"

His blue eyes bored into hers. "I get that you're hurting, Blythe. Yeah, Chloe got sick. Yeah, it stinks. But for you to make Evie sit on the sidelines isn't fair to her."

Splaying her hands across the edge of his desktop, she leaned toward him. "I wasn't—"

Opposite her, he mimicked her stance. "Yes, you were." Though the words were spoken calmly, they weaseled their way into her being, messing with her mind and twisting around her heart.

"I was only trying to protect Evie." Her words were barely a whisper.

"Protect her from what?" He eased around the side

of the desk. "She's been all over Adventure Haven this week. All of the kids have, and nothing happened."

The piles of papers atop his desk seemed to swirl into a single blur. "Yes, it did." She squeezed her eyes shut, willing the threatening tears to remain unshed.

"No, it didn't, Blythe. Everyone is just fine."

Though her eyes were still closed, heat streaked down her cheeks. She was crying. How could that be? She was a master at overcoming her emotions.

"Look at me, Blythe."

Shaking her head, she turned away. She couldn't let him see her tears. No one could. She was strong, capable of keeping everything inside.

"Blythe, you are not responsible for Chloe getting sick."

"Yes, I am." In that instant, the dam she'd built around her heart exploded with a vengeance, unleashing everything she'd tried so hard to keep inside. The pain and guilt sent tears pouring down her face. She would have collapsed had Daniel not been there to catch her.

He eased her into a chair and held her while she sobbed.

"Her mom kept thanking me." She hiccupped. "Hugging me. I didn't...deserve that."

"Yes, you did, Blythe." He set her away from him, forcing her to look at him. "You did nothing wrong. You allowed Chloe to experience camp the way it was meant to be. And you loved her."

Blythe fell silent then, though the tears continued to stream. Daniel was right; she did love Chloe. And Evie. Even though she didn't want to.

Meeting his gaze, she said, "And therein lies the problem."

His eyes searched hers. "What? That you loved her?"

"Yes. If I don't feel, I won't hurt."

He watched her curiously. "Your premise may seem good in theory, but it's almost impossible to execute. Because things like love can't be stopped. God created us to have an abundant life. He wants us to love without condition, just the way He loves us. And I know it can be scary, but that's simply an opportunity to trust God. To understand that whatever the outcome, He's right there with us."

"In case you haven't noticed, trust isn't my strong suit."

"Yes, we've discussed that. However, that may be why God keeps offering you opportunities."

Puffing out a laugh, she swiped her palms over her cheeks, trying to remove the wetness. "I almost hate to admit this, but it does feel better to let it all out." Until this week, she couldn't even remember the last time she'd cried.

"See?"

Her brow lifted. "Were you hoping to make me cry?"

"What are you, nuts? I'm a guy. We hate tears." He smoothed a wayward hair behind her ear, unleashing another wave of emotions she wasn't about to acknowledge. "I just wanted to get to the heart of the problem so we could move forward on a positive note."

She stood then, suddenly needing to put some distance between herself and the good-looking camp director. "Well, you did, so mission accomplished. Now I need to splash some water on my face before I head back to Adventure Haven for some zip-lining with Evie."

His grin carved the slightest dimple into each cheek and she wondered why she hadn't seen them before. She hoped they didn't become a regular occurrence. Otherwise, she'd be in big trouble.

Chapter Eight

Under a crystal blue sky without even a hint of breeze, Daniel waved as the last of the campers pulled away late Saturday morning. Camp Sneffels's inaugural session was officially in the books, and Daniel couldn't be more pleased.

Overall, it had been a successful week, except for the incident with Micah and Chloe's unexpected departure. And much of that success was due to Blythe.

Despite his initial misgivings, he was glad she was here. She had a heart for kids and without her valuable input, he wasn't sure how this week would have turned out.

Besides, he'd really enjoyed getting to know her. The softer side of Blythe was something he suspected very few people ever got to see. She wasn't at all like he'd first imagined. Instead, she was complex and intriguing, and he couldn't seem to find enough excuses to spend more time with her. Like, maybe later this evening.

For now, though, it was time to prepare for round two. Kids aged thirteen to seventeen would arrive tomorrow, and they'd require a different mindset. Taking teens away from their electronic devices for a week meant making sure they were thoroughly entertained. And that was always a challenge.

"Should I move my stuff back to the other cabin?"

In the shade of a pine tree, he turned at the sound of Blythe's voice and simply blinked. "Why would you do that?"

Her brow pinched in confusion. "Because camp is over and I'm back to being just the overseer."

What did she mean, just the overseer? "You mean, you won't be staying on as a camp companion?" It wasn't like Felicia was planning to come back. If Blythe wasn't filling her slot, he'd have to either jockey campers around or come up with another counselor. And considering the campers would be arriving tomorrow, bringing in another companion was going to be tough.

She slid her hands into the back pockets of her jeans. "Why would I? I mean, don't you have another rotation coming in?"

"No, all of our volunteers signed on for two weeks." Something he should have told her when she offered to step into the role. "I just assumed you'd do the same."

"Oh. I was not aware of that."

"That's my fault."

Looking down, she dragged the toe of her sneaker through the gravel. "It's not that I didn't have a great time this week. It was just…" her gaze drifted toward the trees "…more taxing than I'd imagined."

While he understood her hesitation, he was definitely disappointed—and not only because it left him in a bind. Blythe was a great companion, sensitive and caring. "Yeah, I guess the whole thing with Chloe was a little stressful." He shifted from one foot to the other, his mind racing, wondering how quickly he could get an alternate up here.

"It most certainly was that," she said.

Now he had less than twenty-four hours to acquire another companion and make sure they received all of the last-minute training everyone else had gotten. And while such a feat seemed impossible to him, he also knew that nothing was impossible with God. It just meant he wouldn't get to spend any free time with Blythe.

"Yeah, you just go on back to the other cabin. I'll see what I can come up with. Worst case, Allison can split the two extra girls between other companions."

Blythe turned to leave then stopped. "What do you mean? I thought you only had two campers per companion. You make it three, and there could be some discontent, especially with teenage girls. You have an odd number, and somebody is bound to feel left out."

Yet another example of why she fit in here so well.

"Hmm... I hadn't thought of that."

Her brow puckered. "Are you saying that you don't have another backup?"

"Not at all. I have a list of alternates, but whether they're available or not remains to be seen. If they can't get up here right away, I'll have to consider something else."

Chewing her bottom lip, she looked uncharacteristically timid. "May I ask you something?"

"Of course."

Finally, she met his gaze. "What made you want to open a camp for youth cancer patients?"

A laugh puffed out of him before he could stop it. "I can't believe that, in all of our discussions, I've never mentioned the reason behind this camp." Usually he couldn't wait to tell people. Yet even when she'd told him about the camp she went to and how disappointed she'd been, he'd never said a word.

"Follow me." He started toward his office. "You know how I said that I've always been known as the adventurer in my family?"

"Yes." Her short legs moved swiftly to keep up.

"And that my mother had cancer." Stepping onto the porch, he reached for the screen door, holding it open as Blythe moved inside.

"Yes, I remember."

"While she was sick, she asked to go on one of my adventures with me." He moved around his desk and tugged the middle drawer open. "She wasn't really able to travel, so I took her white-water rafting on the Uncompahgre." He reached for the notecard with a columbine on the front. "And she loved every minute of it. Afterward, she told me I had a gift. That I should use it to bring joy to others the way I had with her."

Pausing, he closed the drawer as he sought to hold on to his emotions. "Not long after her death, I started organizing white-water rafting trips for cancer patients. That's how Jack and I first connected. With the foundation's help, we were able to do trips year-round."

"How did you do that? I mean, you can't exactly raft in the winter."

"Well, when it's winter up here, it's summer in South America. Peru and Chile have some of the best white-water rafting anywhere in the world."

"So, these were adults?"

"Yes. But kids were always in the back of my mind. When I thought about all the stuff I got to do when I was little, it made me sad for those who might never have the chance to experience any of that." He eyed the card in his hand. "Anyway, a couple of years ago, after plans for the camp were already in motion, I received this confirmation." He passed the card to Blythe. "My sister-in-law, Carly, found it with my mother's crafting stuff."

Blythe opened it and read aloud. "Daniel, my beautiful baby boy. God has a plan for you. I know you often feel as though you're floundering, wondering what to do with your life, but don't forget who you are. God instilled a love of adventure in you for a reason. I believe it's so you can share that passion with others and bring joy into their lives the way you did mine."

Blythe was blinking rapidly when she looked up at him. "Oh, Daniel."

"My mother is the reason I started this camp, Blythe. If I can bring even a little happiness into these kids' lives…"

She closed the card and a few silent moments ticked by before she said, "What was she like? Your mom."

He took the card from her and returned it to the drawer. "Mona Stephens was amazing. Strong, independent, so full of life. And unbelievably passionate about her faith, family, horses, crafting and community theater."

Blythe let out a soft laugh. "Sounds like she was a really neat lady."

"She was. I only wish she could be here to see that her wish came true."

Blythe's nod was followed by a long stretch of silence. Then, "Daniel?"

He looked at her.

"I'd be honored to serve as a camp companion again."

* * *

Later that afternoon, after camp preparations were complete, the college-age volunteers took off for a movie in Montrose, while others simply wanted to take advantage of the opportunity to rest up before the next day.

Blythe, on the other hand, needed a new pair of shoes. Hiking shoes, to be exact, because while she was ready to take on another week of camp, her sneakers weren't.

After pairing her skinny jeans with a top that was much cuter than the Camp Sneffels T-shirts she'd worn all week and a pair of strappy sandals, she grabbed her leather tote and headed for her car. The stillness of this morning had given way to a whisper of a breeze, leaving them with an almost perfect day.

Clicking the fob to unlock her vehicle, she wondered where she might go to look for the shoes. Considering that this area was a mecca for outdoor enthusiasts, there was bound to be some sort of sports store.

She pulled her phone from her pocket, ready to do a search when she spotted Daniel returning from Adventure Haven. "Just the person I need to see."

He had a large coil of rope slung over his shoulder as he approached. "What's up?"

"I need some hiking shoes. Any suggestions where I might find some?"

"All Geared Up is the place to go for any and all outdoor clothing and equipment. It's right on Main Street in Ouray. Just make your way back to Ridgway, make a right onto Highway 550 and head south. You'll run right into it."

"Sounds easy enough." And with the GPS on her phone to assist…

"It is. Actually…" He rubbed his chin. "Now that I think about it, there are a couple of things I need to pick up there myself. Perhaps we could go together. You ever been to Ouray?"

Why did her insides flutter? "I have not."

"Well then, I'd be negligent if I didn't show you around. And since the chow hall is closed tonight, we could grab a bite to eat while we're there, too. What do you say?"

While part of her was ready to leap at the prospect, the cautious side of her wasn't so sure. After hearing Daniel's story this morning, his reason for starting the camp, she found herself inexplicably drawn to the man. Spending so much time with him, alone no less, could be dangerous. Or completely wonderful.

"Okay, let's do it."

They opted to take Daniel's four-wheel drive SUV rather than her car.

"See that place there on the right?" He pointed after they'd been on the highway for a bit.

She eyed the expanse of land dotted with cattle, set against the backdrop of the mountains. "The one with that big building?"

"That's Noah's rodeo school."

"This is your ranch?" Surprise had her jerking her head to face him.

He chuckled. "It belongs to my dad, but Abundant Blessings Ranch is the only home I've ever known."

She eyed the house and barn in the distance. "You still live there, then?"

"When I'm in town. Though, not for much longer.

With Dad getting married, it's time to find my own place."

"Aww…" She sat back in her seat. "That's sweet that he found love again." Reminded her of those romance novels she read every once in a while. The ones that made her long for things she'd never have. "When's the wedding?"

"Next Saturday."

"Oh, wow. That's coming up quick."

"Yeah, guess you know where I'll be a week from tonight."

She noticed the river winding to her right. "Where are they getting married?"

"At the church we belong to in town. I think Dad would have preferred to get married at the ranch, but his fiancée really wanted a church wedding."

As they drew closer to town, Blythe said, "It feels like the mountains are getting closer." The open range that stretched to the left and right down most of the highway seemed to be shrinking.

"You haven't seen nothin' yet. Just wait until we get into Ouray proper."

Just then she saw the city limit sign. Daniel lowered his speed as he wound left, then right.

"City pool?" She pointed to the complex on her right that boasted a series of pools and water slides.

"That's the hot springs. And unlike some of the others in this part of the state, ours has no sulfur smell."

"Sounds enticing." Something she might need to consider before leaving the area.

"Too bad we didn't bring our suits."

They continued up what she assumed was Main Street. Lined with quaint old buildings, it held the charm of a bygone era. People meandered along the sidewalks, pausing to admire the view. The town was virtually enveloped by the mountains.

"You can tell the high season is upon us." Daniel glanced her way. "Makes it more difficult to find a parking place."

"Ouray is a tourist town?"

He looked at her like she'd sprouted horns. "Don't tell me you've never heard of it."

"Sorry, but no."

"How long have you lived in Colorado?" He turned onto a side street.

"All my life."

"And you've never heard of Ouray?"

"Nope."

Locating a parking space, he simply shook his head. "Ouray is known as the Jeeping Capital of the World *and* the Ice Climbing Capital of the United States. Although, more recently, they've simply dubbed it the Outdoor Recreation Capital of Colorado."

"Which is probably why I've never heard of it." She sent him a knowing look. "But no wonder they have such a great outdoor store."

She stepped out of the vehicle, taking in some of God's finest handiwork. "This is incredible. The mountains…they're, like, right here."

He moved alongside her. "Only a part of what makes Ouray so unique."

Inside the store, where Daniel seemed to know most everyone, including the owners, Blythe found not only the perfect pair of hiking shoes but a couple of cute shirts, a jacket and some shorts. Who knew an outdoor store could have such amazing stuff?

After making their purchases, they ambled up and down the street before making their way back to Daniel's vehicle.

He unlocked the SUV before lifting the hatch. "What are you hungry for?"

"I don't know. What are my options?"

"Pizza, burgers, steak, comfort food—"

"Ah, comfort food sounds great." She deposited her bags.

"Granny's Kitchen it is then."

She lifted a brow. "Granny's Kitchen?"

Locking things back up, he set a hand on the small of her back and urged her across the street. "Trust me, you're gonna love it."

Awareness of his touch sent a wave of warm fuzzies sloshing through her. Comforting and protective, it felt wonderful. Then he removed it to reach for one of the wood-and-glass double doors. Bummer.

Inside, the place had a very cozy feel. The wood-topped counter was lined with stools while cozy booths hugged the wall of windows opposite. And the aromas coming from the kitchen had her mouth watering. Then she spotted the small glass case beside the cash register, which contained some of the biggest chocolate chip cookies she'd ever seen. She might have to get one of those to go.

Locating an open booth, they slipped inside.

"Daniel, what are you doing here, hon?" An older blonde woman eased beside the table and handed them each a menu.

"We're enjoying a little break between camp sessions." He gestured toward Blythe. "Hillary, this is Blythe."

"A pleasure to meet you, Blythe. Are you working at the camp with Daniel?"

"Yes, ma'am."

"All right, I can't wait to hear." Hillary eagerly scooted in beside Daniel. "How did your first week go?"

"Overall, I think it went pretty well." He eyed Blythe across the table. "What do you think?"

"I would have to agree. I think all of the kids had a great time."

"We did have one little girl who had to leave early because she got sick," said Daniel.

"Aww, poor dear." Hillary frowned. "Anything serious?"

"I hope not."

The woman stood then. "What can I get you two to drink?"

After they both requested water, the woman departed, giving them a chance to look at the menu.

"Just so you know," Daniel started, "Hillary is my dad's fiancée."

Blythe couldn't help smiling. "In that case, I'd say your dad's a lucky man."

"What do we have here?" An older man with salt-and-pepper hair approached the table wearing jeans and a denim work shirt, cowboy hat in hand. "You come into town and don't even bother to let your old man know?"

A grinning Daniel shook his head. "Behave, Dad. I have a guest." He turned his attention to her. "Blythe, this ornery cowboy is my father, Clint Stephens."

The man turned his own grin Blythe's way. "That's a very pretty name, young lady."

"Thank you. Would you care to join us?" She scooted over.

"Well…considering I've been waiting all week to hear about camp, I believe I will. If you don't mind."

"I don't mind at all."

The conversation was relaxed and easy. Seemed both Clint and Hillary were very supportive of what Daniel was doing.

When they finally finished their meal—all three of them had settled on the special of roast beef and smashed potatoes, wrapping things up with some homemade peach cobbler—and wound the conversation down, Blythe and Daniel said their goodbyes and headed outside.

To Blythe's disappointment, darkness had already settled over the cute little town she'd hoped to see more of. But as they continued across the street, she couldn't remember the last time she'd had such an enjoyable evening. Simple. Unassuming. Relaxed. "That was fun."

"We give the old man a hard time, but he's a good guy."

"Hillary seems very nice, too."

"She is, but don't let her fool you. She can be a tough cookie. Guess it's a carryover from her days as a big corporate executive."

"Now that's a story I'd like to hear."

"Maybe next time."

Next time?

He paused beside his SUV, reaching for her hand.

Looking into his blue eyes, feeling the warmth of his touch, she swallowed hard. "I didn't really get to see much of the town." The night air surrounding them crackled with energy. She'd never felt anything like it. Nor did she want it to end.

Was Daniel feeling it, too? His gaze seemed fixed on her face, as though memorizing every nuance. "Then I guess we'll just have to do this again."

Chapter Nine

Daniel had campers arriving in three hours. So why was he sitting in the chow hall, nursing a second cup of coffee when he should be roaming the camp, making sure everything was ready?

Because he had yet to see any sign of Blythe.

Seemed every time they were alone together, something sparked between him and the woman who held the fate of Camp Sneffels in her hands. And he was drawn to her like a bee to pollen.

No doubt about it, he was falling for Blythe. However, if he were falling, that meant there was still hope he could catch himself. But he was way beyond that. He'd already fallen. Hard.

He scrubbed a hand over his clean-shaven face. How could that be possible? It hadn't even been two weeks since they met. Then again, Blythe had gone through quite a transformation in that same amount of time.

That day she'd arrived at Camp Sneffels, she was like a tightly closed bud, its true beauty hidden, sealed off from the world. Then, slowly but surely, she began to emerge from her protected state, blooming into a beautiful flower, something rare and precious that had captivated him.

In his twenty-eight years on this earth, he'd never met anyone like her. Nor anyone who seemed to consume his thoughts the way she did.

Presenting him with a major dilemma.

He really wanted to spend time with Blythe and get to know her better. But was it appropriate? Blythe was still the overseer for the Ridley Foundation, after all. What if she thought he was simply trying to get into her good graces so she'd write a favorable report on the camp and, in turn, continue its funding?

His entire being groaned as he took another swig from his cup. How stupid could he be?

Was he glad he hadn't kissed her. Not that he hadn't wanted to. Matter of fact, it had taken everything in him *not* to kiss her. The way her remarkable eyes sparkled in the moonlight…boy, was he in trouble.

"How was your date?" Levi plopped down in a chair on the opposite side of the table.

Daniel's gut tightened. "What date?"

"You and Blythe. I saw you two drive in last night. Kind of late, if you ask me."

"It was barely ten o'clock. And it was not a date. She needed some hiking shoes, so I ran her into Ouray."

"It took you four hours to pick out shoes?"

Actually, it was more like five, but how did Levi know that? "Look, I know you're fishin', Levi, but I ain't biting."

"Fine, go ahead and deny it, but I know you have feelings for her." His smug grin grated on Daniel.

"And how would you know that?"

"Uh, because I've known *you* since kindergarten." He twisted his Camp Sneffels ball cap backward. "You don't go crazy for the chicks. But the way you look at Blythe…that's the kind of stuff you'd find in one of them romance novels."

"Oh, so you've taken up reading?" Daniel may have appeared calm, but inside he was tap-dancing around landmines.

"No, but my mom has, like, hundreds of those things lying around her house."

"Maybe you should borrow one. Might help you get a date instead of spying on other people."

"Hey, I wasn't spying." His friend looked almost indignant. "I just happened to be outside, that's all. And why are you treating me like the enemy? I think it'd be great if you and Blythe got together."

Yeah, if the future of Camp Sneffels didn't rest in her hands.

Grabbing his now-empty coffee cup, Daniel stood just as Blythe walked inside, her tablet tucked under her arm. And for some reason, Daniel couldn't help but stare. Her hair was down for once, the soft waves skimming her shoulders. And the slight smile that played at her lips when she saw him tangled his insides like a bowl full of spaghetti.

A strong hand clapped against his shoulder, interrupting his reverie.

"Well, lookie there," said Levi. "It appears you're not the only one who's mastered that smitten look." He gave Daniel a final squeeze. "Have fun. I'm off to inspect the zip line."

"Is there a problem?" Daniel managed to give his adventure director his full attention.

"No. Just routine stuff." Levi started for the door. "Like you always say, safety first."

Watching his friend leave, Daniel could only shake his head. Levi knew him too well. Lord willing, no one else would be able to read him as easily as Levi. Especially Blythe.

He scanned the space where at least half of the staff and volunteers were scattered about, either finishing breakfast, engaged in conversation or quietly contemplating the day. Then he spotted Blythe, sitting at a corner table by herself.

Had Levi scared her away, or was she avoiding Daniel? Could it be that she was having regrets about last night, too? Not that he regretted any of it. His time with her had been amazing. It was his growing feelings that troubled him.

With a bolstering breath, he crossed to where she sat. "Good morning."

"Morning." She smiled up at him, a hint of pink in her cheeks.

Unable to look away, he said, "Are you okay? I mean, you're sitting all by yourself."

"I'm fine. I just needed to make some notes for my report." She motioned to her tablet on the wooden tabletop.

Funny, he'd never seen her do that before. Why did she feel the need to do it now?

Maybe she's writing about the camp director who tried to schmooze her.

He wasn't trying to schmooze her.

"I see you're wearing your new hiking shoes."

She noted her footwear. "I never imagined they'd be so comfortable."

"You got a good brand. They'll last you a long time."

She reached for her coffee. "Thank you again for introducing me to All Geared Up. I might need to stop in there before I leave. There were a couple of sundresses I can't stop thinking about."

Great. While she was thinking about sundresses, he was thinking how great she'd look in those sundresses.

"Well, I need to go check in with Levi. Make sure Adventure Haven is ready to go. I'll talk to you later."

He turned and dashed out of the building, wondering who that had been talking back there. He'd sounded like an idiot. Nobody talked like that unless they were nervous or trying to escape.

You were doing both, buddy.

Grr... He'd never met anyone who had this kind of effect on him. Why couldn't he stop thinking about her?

Because you like her.

He sighed. That was a fact. That didn't mean it was right, though. She played a big role in determining if Camp Sneffels would live to see another year. So what if she was pretty and fun to be with and got along great with his dad and Hillary and probably the rest of his family, too? He'd just have to do his best to steer clear of Blythe. Because every time he looked into her eyes, he'd remember what a good time they'd had together and how much he couldn't wait to be with her again.

But he had campers arriving soon, and his focus needed to be on them.

Blythe watched the door close behind Daniel, wondering why he was behaving so strangely. Not at all like the man who'd stood mere inches from her last night, staring deeply into her eyes while her traitorous mind played a continuous loop of what-ifs.

No, just now he'd been distant. Disconnected.

Then again, a new crop of campers would be arriving

soon, and the kids were his top priority. Still, he could have at least mentioned something about last night. Said that he'd had a good time. Yet, except for commenting on her shoes, he'd avoided the subject altogether, and for some reason, that bugged her.

I didn't hear you talking about last night, either.

That was not true. She'd thanked him and mentioned the sundresses.

He didn't offer to take her again.

And that bothers you why?

Good question. Because she certainly wasn't interested in a relationship. Not with Daniel or anyone else. Besides, next week at this time, she'd be on her way back to Denver where she would remain while Daniel was still out here.

Giving herself a stern shake, she turned her attention to her tablet. She'd jotted down some notes from the first week of camp while they were fresh in her mind. Despite the bears, Micah's disappearance and Chloe's illness, things had gone incredibly well. No camp was perfect, she knew that. Yet Daniel's attention to detail had ensured that Camp Sneffels met the needs of every child. If only she and Miranda had been so fortunate as to attend a camp like this.

Her phone buzzed then, and Jenna's image appeared on the screen.

Only then did it dawn on Blythe that she hadn't been in touch with her sister since the day she arrived, so, naturally, she accepted the call. "Good morning."

"Well, you're awful chipper." Jenna sounded surprised.

"What's not to be chipper about?" She closed the cover on her tablet and shoved it aside. "I'm smack-dab in the middle of some of the most beautiful country you've ever seen. Camp Sneffels is gorgeous." Not to mention the camp director.

"So, you've been too busy taking in the scenery to give me a call? I haven't heard from you in over a week. What's going on?"

"Sorry about that. But yes, I have been busy." Leaning back against the wooden chair, she peered outside the window where aspens and pines were bathed in golden sunlight. This was going to be a beautiful day. "I ended up taking on a role as camp counselor when one of the other gals started battling some pretty bad morning sickness."

"Why would she agree to serve as a counselor in her first trimester? I mean, some folks get really sick. Including yours truly."

"It wasn't her fault, Jenna." Blythe reached for her coffee cup. "She didn't know she was pregnant until she started getting sick. And she only found out because the camp doctor had her do a pregnancy test." Blythe took a sip.

"Oh. But why did you have to step in? Didn't the beach bum have some backups?"

Beach bum? Blythe almost laughed out loud. Her thoughts on Daniel had definitely changed since she first arrived.

"He did, but I volunteered anyway."

"Why would you do that?" Jenna sounded appalled.

"Because I like kids. And I wanted to make sure they had the best camp experience possible." She purposely left off the part about having access to everything behind the scenes. That would only bring on more questions.

"Unlike yours, way back when," replied Jenna.

"Definitely."

"Okay, I get that, but I still have a hard time envisioning you as a camp counselor. You're not exactly the outdoorsy type, Blythe."

Blythe felt herself smile as she perused her fellow volunteers. "You'd be quite surprised what all I've done this week. Hiking, fishing, zip-lining—"

"*You* zip-lined?"

"On more than one occasion." Pride sifted through her. "Not only that, I found it *very* freeing."

"I'm sorry, but who are you and what have you done with my sister, Blythe?"

She couldn't help laughing. Jenna knew all too well that Blythe preferred to play things safe. "Deciding to serve as a counselor, or companion, as Daniel prefers to call us, was the best decision I've made in a long time."

"Daniel? Beach bum guy?"

She still cringed when she thought about her initial reaction. "Yeah, I may have been a little harsh in my original assessment of him."

"I don't know. Judging from that picture you sent me, I'd say you were spot-on."

"Let's just say he cleans up well." Quite well, actually.

"Good-looking, huh?"

"Yes, but more than that, he has a huge heart for these kids. He wants nothing more than for them to have fun and to forget that they have cancer."

"Sounds like he's won you over. But then, it is in his best interests."

Blythe fingered the empty sweetener packet on the table. "What do you mean?"

"Well, you do hold the purse strings for his camp.

To a point anyway. But without your approval, he likely won't have a camp next year."

Blythe's insides tensed as she began to realize what her sister was insinuating. "You think he's using me?"

"Not using you. Just putting on a good face."

Indignation stiffened her spine. "For your information, that's one of the reasons I wanted to be a counselor. So I'd be fully aware of everything that went on in the camp."

"No need to get snippy."

She sucked in a calming breath. "I'm not getting snippy. I just don't appreciate you underestimating me."

"I wasn't underestimating you. I'm just…cautious."

"Seriously? You're trying to claim *my* label?"

"All right, I'm a realist."

"That's better." Palming her cup, Blythe swirled its remaining contents. "And yes, you are. One of the things I've always appreciated about you. You never tried to keep things from me the way Mom did."

"Only part of the reason she and I always butted heads where you were concerned."

"She was just trying to protect me. But thanks for looking out for me."

"Hey, I'm your big sister. Nobody's going to tangle with you but me."

"I know. But hey, I need to go, Jenna." Blythe shoved her chair back and stood. "The next round of campers will be pulling in shortly, and I need to be ready. Teenagers this week."

"Oh, I'll definitely be praying for you, then."

She ended the call and took her cup and plate to the kitchen before gathering her tablet and heading outside. The sun's warmth beat down on her as she crossed the grassy area around the flagpole. At this rate, it would be downright hot by this afternoon.

Continuing onto the dirt path, she found herself annoyed by Jenna's lack of faith in her. Did she really think Blythe would let Daniel take advantage of her like that? Or anybody else, for that matter. She supposed it was her fault, though. She should have kept her thoughts to herself that first day instead of running off at the mouth. Now Jenna had a negative impression of Daniel, one that couldn't be further from the truth.

Just then, she saw the man in question moving in her direction.

"Just the person I wanted to see." She slowed as he approached. "I forgot to ask you about the Welcome Roundup. Do you need some help getting things ready?"

"Actually, I think Allison has everything under control. But you're welcome to ask her." He moved past her. "Sorry, I gotta run."

Why was Daniel acting so weird today? Not at all like the man who'd offered to drive her into Ouray and then showed her a positively wonderful evening.

Without your approval, he likely won't have a camp next year. Jenna's words returned to taunt her.

Suddenly, Blythe found herself questioning why Daniel had asked to join her when she went into town when he'd already given her directions. It wasn't like Ouray or the store was difficult to find. She would have been fine on her own. He was the one who'd insisted on showing her around and stopping for dinner. And it had been a perfectly wonderful evening. Until today.

As much as she hated to admit it, perhaps Jenna was right. Maybe the handsome camp director had ulterior motives.

Chapter Ten

Daniel stumbled out of the camp office Tuesday morning, feeling more than a little ragged. But it had nothing to do with the kids. Sure, teenagers were different than the younger kids, moodier and such, but they all seemed excited to be here. Happy to hang out with others who were just like them, instead of being singled out as the kid with cancer. Here they were just another camper.

He rubbed the back of his neck. No, he couldn't blame his lack of sleep on them. Instead, his annoyance rested on the fact that he hadn't talked to Blythe since Sunday morning. That was, if you could call their brief back-and-forth talking.

Okay, so he'd been trying to steer clear of her, hoping to avoid any conflict of interest. He'd just never imagined it would be so difficult. Especially when she seemed to be avoiding him, too. Whenever he crossed her line of vision, she looked the other way. That stung.

Blowing out a frazzled breath, he peered up at a hazy blue sky. He couldn't speak for Blythe, but he'd really enjoyed her company Saturday night. It was nice to see what she was like outside of work. That night, they'd been just two people having fun. Maybe even growing attracted to each other. At least he was. So unless he wanted to go out of his ever-lovin' mind, he'd better find a way to remedy this situation now.

Before he could reach the chow hall, the sound of gravel crunching under tires had him turning to see a deputy sheriff's vehicle moving slowly up the drive. A second glance verified the driver was, indeed, the third oldest Stephens brother, Matt.

Daniel did an about-face and greeted Matt as he stepped out of his Tahoe. "What's up, bro?"

"Not too much." Matt shook Daniel's extended hand before reeling him in for a brotherly hug. "Kinda miss seein' you around," he said as they parted.

"Yeah, well, I've been keeping pretty busy up here."

"I can see that." Matt eyed a group of teenagers headed to breakfast.

Daniel watched his brother. "Did you come up here on business or out of curiosity?"

"Maybe a little bit of both. Thought it would be nice to see the place the way it's meant to be."

Two teen girls ran past, giggling.

"Looks like everyone's having fun," said Matt.

"I think so." Daniel settled his hands on his hips. "How's my newest niece doing?" His family had grown by leaps and bounds in the past two years. All four of his older brothers had married, and in addition to his other nieces and nephews, they'd welcomed three babies in less than a year. The latest, Matt's second daughter, Riley, had been born only three weeks ago.

Matt beamed like the proud father he was. "Good. Lacie's finally getting her bearings, too." He shoved his hands into the pockets of his cargo pants. "I gotta tell you, since I missed out on this part of Kenzie's life, I really enjoyed getting to be home with them those first two weeks."

Matt hadn't learned about his daughter Kenzie until she was five, but she'd been the light of his life from the moment he found out about her.

"Ah, you were just glad you didn't have to go in to work."

"Yeah, whatever. Speaking of work, I thought I'd let you know there's a wildfire that's cropped up about thirty-five miles west of here."

Daniel's gaze drifted to the sky. "Guess that explains the haze."

Matt nodded. "Weather service is calling for some high winds tomorrow. Lord willing, they'll get it under control by then. Figured I'd give you a heads-up, though. Just in case."

"Is it headed this way?"

"Not at the moment, but you know that can change on a dime. If those winds start coming out of the west, you're going to be inundated with smoke. And when you're dealing with cancer patients—"

"Yeah, I hear ya." Daniel scrubbed a hand over his face. "We have our evacuation plan. I just pray we don't have to use it."

"Emergency management is already on it," Matt added. "They're prepping the school, just in case."

Ouray only had one school, which served preschool through twelfth grade students. Still, it had a gymnasium, kitchen, bathrooms...

"That's good."

Out of the corner of his eye, he saw Blythe moving across the grass with another companion and their campers. When she saw him, her brow furrowed. She said something to her fellow companion, then started his way, her ponytail swaying with each determined step while the others continued on to the chow hall.

Man, did she look good. Though he still preferred her hair down.

"What's going on?" Her pretty eyes moved between Daniel and his brother.

Then he realized Matt was in uniform and his vehicle was visible for all to see.

"Blythe, this is my brother Matt."

One optimistic brow lifted. "Does this mean you're not here in an official capacity?"

Matt looked from Blythe to Daniel, seemingly not knowing what to say.

"It's okay. I keep Blythe informed of everything that happens here at the camp." Even when he didn't want to.

"I was just telling Daniel about a wildfire to the west of here."

"How far away?"

"About thirty-five miles."

Like Daniel, she glanced toward the sky. "I thought things were looking kind of strange today. Is there anything we need to do?"

"Not at the moment. I'll keep Daniel updated on the situation, though."

"Yes, please do." Again, she lifted her gaze. "We don't want these kids breathing a bunch of smoke that has who knows what in it. Their immune systems are already compromised."

"I understand." Matt turned his attention to Daniel. "I'll be in touch."

"All right." He waved as his brother opened the door of his vehicle. "Take care."

As Matt pulled away, Daniel could feel Blythe watching him.

"What do we do now?" she finally asked.

He lifted a shoulder. "We're at the mercy of nature, so there's not much we can do but wait and see."

"You know that's not my favorite option."

The remark made him grin. "Mine, either. Worst case scenario, we have an evacuation plan in place."

"I remember going over it. Though I never expected we'd have to use it."

"Hopefully, we won't. But like I said, we have to be prepared for anything out here."

She nodded, concern evident in her expression.

Feeling as excited as he was nervous to have her beside him once again, he said, "How are things going? We haven't talked in a while. Are you and your girls doing all right?"

She smiled, her features relaxing. "They're great. Typical teenagers. Lots of giggles and talk about boys."

"I've missed you." The words were out of his mouth before he could stop them. Unable to take them back, he figured he might as well go for it. "If you find yourself in need of some chamomile tea to help you sleep, I'm happy to help." He'd come to enjoy those late-night talks in his office.

She looked away then, but not before he glimpsed the pink in her cheeks. "With so much activity, I'm pretty much asleep as soon as my head hits the pillow these days."

Disappointment wove its way through him.

Until she peered up at him through long lashes

that only made him want to be with her more. "I'll be sure and keep that in mind, though."

What was wrong with her?

Blythe had had no problem sleeping for the past week and a half. Yet tonight, she couldn't seem to keep her eyes closed. Probably because every time she did, she saw Daniel looking at her, saying he missed her. Why did he have to sound so sincere?

Maybe because he was.

Rolling onto her side, she punched her pillow. Truth be told, she missed spending time with him, too. So, what was the problem?

Ah, yes. Daniel had been acting weird Sunday morning. Yet rather than discussing it with him, she'd let Jenna sway her with her assumptions.

And to think, Daniel had talked about making another trip to Ouray. Together. Now Blythe doubted that would ever happen.

You could ask him.

And sound desperate? No way. She shouldn't even care. After all, she usually steered clear of romantic entanglements, saving her heart the pain of a breakup later when whoever she fell in love with decided he didn't want to be with a woman who might not be able to give him children. True, she'd only had radiation treatments and not chemo, leaving her with a fifty-fifty chance of conceiving. But better to anticipate being in the fifty percent that couldn't conceive than find herself in a shambles later when the man she loved decided she was less than a woman.

Been there, done that. A hard lesson, but one that had taught her well.

Not all guys are like that.

So she'd been told. But she'd managed to find one that was, leaving her skeptical of all the others.

Except Daniel *was* different. Maybe that was part of the problem. Daniel made her want to throw caution to the wind. Dared her to dream of happily-ever-afters and actually believe they were possible.

Talk about an adventure.

Noticing once again that Teri was still staring at her phone, the way she had every other night, Blythe finally gave in to the strong desire for a cup of tea. She told Teri she was stepping out for a while, donned a sweatshirt, grabbed a tea bag and headed outside. Who knew? Daniel might not even be awake. Which would be fine. Although, for her own sanity, some tea would really hit the spot.

Making her way up the dirt path illuminated only by a single uber bright light between the chow hall and Daniel's office, she tried to determine if Daniel was still up. There was a light on in the office portion of the building, but it was rather dim.

Her steps slowed. Maybe she should just go back.

Eyeing the chow hall, she recalled the bears that had been there the previous week. Her heart thumped against her ribs. She was out here all alone.

Just then she heard a twig snap somewhere in the darkness. Her body tensed, her pulse skyrocketing. What if—?

"Blythe?"

Fists balled, she choked back a scream as Daniel came into view. Air whooshed out of her lungs as she whispered, "What are you doing out here?"

"Making my nightly rounds. I have to make sure everything and everyone is secure. What are you doing?"

"Um." She huffed and puffed as though she'd just run a marathon.

"Are you okay? Were you jogging or something?"

Straightening, she blew out a final breath and tried to compose herself. This was such a bad idea.

"No. I was—" tucking her hair behind her ear, she peered up at him "—just having a difficult time sleeping, that's all."

The corners of his mouth lifted in a knowing manner. "Come on. Let's head to my office."

She followed quietly, her insides tangled like the heap of wires behind her TV.

Once they were inside, Daniel filled a cup with water and put it in the microwave to heat without even asking if that was what she wanted, which gave her a warm, fuzzy feeling. It had been a long time since anyone had anticipated her needs.

When he turned her way, he had an almost shy look about him. "I didn't think you'd come." His smile bordered on nervousness. "But I'm glad you did."

"Oh?" Her heart stuttered as she inched toward the long counter where he stood.

"I'm sorry I've been acting like a jerk lately."

Okay, she wasn't expecting that. "What? No, you're not jerk. You're just busy, that's all."

The timer beeped.

He retrieved the cup and handed it to her. "No, I'm a jerk. I've been avoiding you on purpose."

So, she hadn't been the only one. Dropping her tea bag into the hot water, she said, "Why would you do that?"

"Because we had such a great time Saturday night."

Wrapping her fingers around the warm cup, she arched a brow.

"I was afraid you might think it was all an act," he added.

"What do mean, an act?"

"You're the overseer for the foundation funding my camp. I'm the camp director."

"I see." Daniel and Jenna must think along the same wavelength. Still holding the cup, she bobbed the tea bag. "Did you think you could, somehow, sway my opinion?"

He shook his head. "Not at all. Never even blipped on my radar. Until Sunday morning."

"What happened then?" She blew into the steaming liquid.

Raking a hand through his short blond hair, he started toward his desk and away from her. "You've been such an asset to me here at the camp. And watching you emerge from your protected cocoon and seeing the beautiful butterfly you truly are has been one of the greatest thrills of my life. I find myself longing to being with you, Blythe." He faced her then. "Then, Saturday, we connected on a different level, which made me wonder if us spending time alone together could be a conflict of interest—not that I don't trust you to be professional."

While one part of her relaxed, the other was practically giddy. Not only did he like her, she'd given the adventurer one of the greatest thrills of his life.

"For the record, I had fun, too." She watched him over the top of her cup. "Just in case you couldn't tell." She took a tiny sip, the drink hot on her tongue. "If there is any conflict of interest, I'm as much to blame as anyone. But I think we're fine."

Fine? In case you've forgotten, there's a reason you avoid relationships.

"Good." Daniel smiled in earnest. "Because there's something I'd like to ask you."

There went her heart again, ignoring any and all logic. "What's that?"

"Would you accompany me to my dad and Hillary's wedding Saturday night?" He looked suddenly relieved. As though he'd been dying to ask the question but was too afraid.

She knew she should say no. She hadn't had a date in forever, mostly because she avoided them like the plague. But the thought of spending another evening with Daniel was too hard to resist. "I would like that very much."

Chapter Eleven

~⚘~

Daniel tried not to think about the wildfire as he drifted off to sleep that night. Instead, he focused on the fact that Blythe had agreed to be his date for the wedding. Coming clean with her, telling her how he really felt, had been the right thing to do. After all, he couldn't help it if he was drawn to her. Now, with everything out in the open, they were free to spend time together without worrying about motives.

A smoky haze dimmed what should have been a brilliant sun as he emerged from his sleeping quarters the next morning. Fortunately, he had a plan. Because his goal was to make sure these kids had fun, no matter what.

Only a few staff members were in the chow hall when he entered. They waved in greeting as Daniel made his way to the kitchen where the aromas of bacon and sausage awakened his appetite.

"Juanita, my favorite chef in the whole wide world."

The woman appeared skeptical as she looked up from the griddle. "Mr. Daniel, you cannot sweet-talk me." She wielded her turner like a weapon.

"Now why would you think I'm trying to sweet talk you?" He paused beside her.

"Because you look hungry. And we are not serving breakfast until the children are here."

"Oh, so you think I'm in here looking for handouts?" He glanced at the golden disks atop the griddle.

"Aren't you?" Dark eyes narrowed on him.

"Well, while I am starving and would be more than happy to accept any offer of food—" crossing his arms over his chest, he leaned against the stainless-steel work table "—I'm actually here to make sure you're cool with the plan for today." A plan that would allow the kids to partake in adventures until the smoke forced them inside. Once that happened, the staff was all set to go with games, movies, even karaoke and a dance party.

"Oh, yes." She smiled then, moving the pancakes to the warming tray. "We will have sandwiches, chips and fruit for lunch. Things we can easily package and bring to the children while they play." She spooned more pancake batter onto the griddle. It sizzled, sending a waft of sweetness into the air. "Then we have party food—popcorn, nachos, ice cream—when they come inside, and I already make enchilada casserole for dinner."

"Wow! You planned all that, *and* you've already made the casserole? Were you here all night?"

Juanita chuckled. "I plan it all in my head when I drive home last night. Then I make the casserole this morning." She lifted a shoulder. "It's good to have helpers."

"Oh, yeah." Sometimes he forgot that Juanita had staff assisting her in the kitchen. "I appreciate you being so accommodating. Especially since I didn't give you much notice."

"Things happen. That wildfire is not good. But we make the most of a bad situation."

Slipping an arm around her shoulders, he said, "Thank you, Juanita." The volume in the dining room seemed to be increasing. "Guess I'd better let you get back to work. Sounds like the natives are getting restless."

When he returned to the dining hall, his gaze was promptly drawn to the cowboy on the other side of the room. While kids scurried to find their seats, Daniel continued toward his eldest brother, Noah.

"What's up, big brother? You don't usually join us for breakfast."

A smile formed creases around his brother's dark eyes. "Figured if your plan was to let these kids play as much as possible, I'd best be here to get the horses on the trail early."

Daniel was still amazed by the amount of support his family had given him, especially when Noah had his own business to run. "Thanks, man. Now why don't you pull up a chair and let me buy you some breakfast?"

Noah removed his straw cowboy hat. "Have you ever known me to turn down Juanita's cooking?"

"No, I have…" His words trailed off as Blythe entered with her two campers. The smile she sent him moved across the room and straight to his heart. Man, she was pretty.

"So that's the young lady Dad told us about."

Daniel's smile evaporated. He jerked his head to see Noah staring at Blythe. "What did he say?"

His brother shrugged. "You know how the old man is."

That was precisely what had Daniel concerned. Clint

Stephens was becoming quite adept at matchmaking, having honed his skills with Andrew and his wife, Carly, before moving on to Matt and Lacie, Noah and Lily and, finally, Jude and Kayla. Now he no doubt had his sights set on Daniel and Blythe. And while Daniel was definitely interested in Blythe, he wasn't quite sure how he felt about his father's meddling.

Good thing they were here at the camp where the odds of running into Dad were slim to none.

"Which reminds me," Noah said. "He's coming up here to help me today."

"What?"

"He's bringing a few more horses, too. Figured it would allow us to get more kids on the trail with two of us working."

Note to self: keep Blythe as far away from Dad as possible.

Just then, his father swung open the door to the chow hall and moved inside. Unfortunately, the group of kids crowded between Daniel and the entrance made it impossible for him to intercept the man.

Peering over the heads of the kids, Daniel cringed when he saw Blythe approach his father. They smiled and chatted. Blythe laughed at something the old man said, ratcheting Daniel's unease. Finally, she pointed in Daniel and Noah's direction. Dad smiled and nodded as she walked away.

"That Blythe sure is a sweet thing," his father said when Daniel finally caught up to him. "Pretty, too."

And so it begins. "Appreciate you coming to help out." With the horses anyway.

"It's the least I can do. 'Specially now that Mother

Nature's gone and thrown a monkey wrench into things."

One of the helpers from the kitchen set a platter of pancakes and meat on their table. The young woman addressed Daniel. "Juanita said you guys should eat first so you can get to work."

The three men glanced across the dining hall to see a smiling Juanita waving from the kitchen.

"Well, I'll be." Daniel's father waved back.

Daniel pulled out his chair and sat down to eat. "Sometimes I think that woman can read my mind." Because the faster Dad was out of the way, the less Daniel had to worry about him interacting with Blythe.

So, when his father and Noah polished off their breakfast almost before the kids had even started eating and headed outside to unload horses, Daniel was pleased.

While the kids ate, Daniel seized the opportunity to announce that campers would be allowed to participate in unlimited adventures that morning, which brought him a round of cheers.

He went on to tell them about the wildfires, assuring them they were in no danger. He informed them he had a brother who was a sheriff's deputy and that he was keeping an eye on the situation. "However, the smoke may be an issue later. If it becomes a problem, we'll simply move the fun in here." He gestured around the chow hall. "If it's not a problem, then you guys are free to have fun all day."

Another round of cheers had him smiling, however his optimism waned an hour or so after lunch as the smell of smoke began to accompany the ever-increasing haze. Moving about Adventure Haven, he eyed the once-blue sky. The sun's rays were now blocked by a layer of brown smoke.

"How's it going?"

He turned at the sweet sound of Blythe's voice. "Not too bad, considering." He pointed toward the sky. "The kids are still running around and enjoying themselves."

"As they should be." Her smile had him feeling as though all was right with the world.

Shifting his focus to the kids tackling the challenge course, he said, "What have you been up to?"

"Horseback riding with your father."

He jerked to face her.

"He's pretty funny, you know."

Yeah, hilarious. "How so?"

"Just telling the kids stories."

He shifted from one foot to the other. "What kind of stories?"

"Oh, just some historical things about the area. Of course, whether they're true or not is debatable. And then he talked about you and your brothers." One perfectly arched brow lifted then, along with the corners of her mouth. "I learned quite a bit about you."

He couldn't help wincing. "Such as…?"

"Daniel?"

He looked past Blythe to see Dr. Joel coming their way.

"Hey, doc. What's going on?"

"I'm afraid it's the air. We've got a lot of particles starting to filter down. This would be a good time to bring the kids inside."

Even though he'd anticipated this, Daniel's heart broke. Everyone was having so much fun. "If you think that's best, then yes, of course we'll bring them in." He grabbed the radio clipped to the pocket of his cargo shorts, raised it to his lips and pressed the button. "Attention! All campers and faculty are to report to the chow hall immediately." He repeated the directive as Blythe moved to retrieve her campers from the challenge course. "Thanks, doc."

"I hate to be the bearer of bad news—" Dr. Joel scanned the horizon "—but some things just can't be helped."

"I understand."

Daniel helped herd the kids back to the chow hall, only to find Matt's vehicle parked outside of the camp office. Leaning toward Blythe, he whispered, "This doesn't look good."

Worry creased her brow, though her smile told him she was trying to remain positive. "I'll get the kids to the chow hall. You go talk to your brother and find out what's going on."

Inside his office, he found not only Matt, but Dad and Noah gathered around his desk. "I don't suppose this is just a family meeting, is it?"

"Sorry, Daniel." Matt shook his head. "Fire's still a good ways off, but the winds are increasing, blowing all that smoke right toward the camp. It's time to evacuate."

The look on Daniel's face when he announced to the kids that they had to evacuate the camp nearly broke Blythe's heart. And while the kids were, no doubt, disappointed, did they realize how badly Daniel ached for them? Having to tear them away from this place they had so looked forward to attending only days into their adventure must have been excruciatingly difficult for him.

How she wished she could be with him now, assisting him as he called parents to notify them of the evacuation. But that wasn't her job. Instead, she was in her cabin, making sure the girls stayed on task, packing their belongings so everyone would be ready when the buses arrived.

She and Teri had already packed their things. Now they stood watch in one wing of the cabin, allowing the other companions to pack while the two of them did their best to make sure the campers left nothing behind.

Surprisingly, the girls were going about their tasks virtually in silence. The tension in the room was almost palpable, though. Or maybe it was just that it was growing warm. They'd closed all of the windows because of the smoke, and with everyone in there, things had grown stuffy fast.

In an effort to help alleviate things, Blythe swung open the door at the far end of the room, allowing a small amount of air to flow through the screen.

"I don't get it." Anger laced the fifteen-year-old girl's words as she begrudgingly shoved a wad of clothing into her duffle bag. "If the fire's not coming this way, then why do we have to leave?"

"It's not about the fire, Jessica." Blythe understood their frustration. "It's because of the smoke. We can't risk anyone getting sick."

"This stinks," mumbled a sixteen-year-old wearing a scarf over her bald head. "And I'm not talking about the smoke."

Evidently it had only taken one person opening her mouth to get the ball rolling. Then again, Blythe supposed they just needed to vent.

"I know it does." Teri did her best to empathize with

the girl. Not that she had to try very hard, because she was just as frustrated as everyone else. Something the girls couldn't seem to understand.

"They said we were going to have fun." Another young lady scowled, rolling up her sleeping bag.

"Yeah, we didn't even get to have our party," added a discontented fourteen-year-old, slamming the lid on the wooden chest at the foot of her bed for emphasis.

Unfortunately, the move only made Blythe's blood boil. These girls had no idea the lengths Daniel had gone to for them. Every worker at this camp, for that matter.

It's simply their disappointment talking.

Yes, but they were blaming Daniel when the circumstances were completely out of his control.

"I can't believe they're making us leave," the first girl flopped onto her bare mattress.

Blythe's body tensed, her pulse pounding in her ears. She couldn't believe they were going on like this. It was one thing to voice your disappointment, but it was just plain mean to cast blame as though someone was purposely doing this to them.

They're just kids.

No, they were teenagers. Old enough to know better. And after what she'd gone through, she was not about to let this trash talk continue.

"Daniel's just afraid he's going to get into trouble," blabbed another, clueless as to what she was talking about.

"That's *enough*!"

The girls looked at Blythe, wide-eyed.

"Do you have any idea how hard this is on Daniel?" Her glare moved from one girl to the next. "How deeply he wants you to have fun?" And the next. "He's worked for years to put this camp together. Do you know why?"

All of them slowly shook their heads, obviously stunned by her outburst.

"Because he wanted you guys to have a place to escape. A place to have fun and feel normal, instead of being treated like sick kids all the time."

The girl with the scarf crossed her arms over her chest. "Like you'd know what that's like." Her comment flew all over Blythe like white on rice.

"Actually, I do." After leveling her gaze on that particular young lady, she paced the length of the room like a drill sergeant. "I was thirteen when I was diagnosed with cancer. My parents sheltered me, wanting to protect me." Hands clasped behind her back, she turned on her heel and continued across the wooden floor in the other direction. "Then I finally got to go to a camp where they promised me all kinds of fun. Except they didn't deliver, because they didn't care." She faced them again. "Daniel cares about each and every one of you kids. The last thing he wants is for you to be disappointed. This evacuation wasn't his choice, and it's breaking his heart for us to have to leave. So, I suggest you try to be a little more understanding."

"Everything okay in there?" The sound of Daniel's voice stopped her in her tracks.

She whirled to find him standing just outside the cabin door.

Her heart thudded. Mostly because she had yet to calm down from her tirade.

"I don't know." She glanced back at the girls. "Is everything all right, ladies?"

"Yes, ma'am." The first girl jumped to her feet.

"Yes." The second nodded.

"Blythe, could I see you out here, please?"

Her insides cringed. Daniel had obviously heard her rant. Served her right for opening the door. No telling what he was going to say.

She marched outside, closing the door behind her so the girls couldn't eavesdrop. After all, if she was in trouble, she certainly didn't want them to hear.

As soon as Daniel saw her, he began walking, obviously moving them away from prying eyes. "That was quite a performance in there."

She fell in beside him. "Not very professional, I know."

Hands shoved in his pockets, he said, "Actually, I thought you handled them quite well."

She stopped beside a towering pine. "Really? How much did you hear?"

"Enough to know you were defending me." He faced her then, his expression unreadable. "Which was totally unnecessary."

"You didn't hear all the stuff they were saying in there. This evacuation isn't your fault. They have no right to take it out on you."

"They're teenagers. They complain about everything."

Crossing her arms, she puffed out a laugh. "That doesn't make it right. Not after all you've done for them."

He smiled then, touching a hand to her cheek. "Knowing you believe in my efforts is enough for me."

Her anxiety eased as she leaned into his touch. "You have been tested, and your heart is pure."

Without the slightest hesitation, he tugged her closer

and kissed her. Softly, gently… Talk about a pleasant surprise. One that ended way too quickly.

Taking a step back, he said, "I came by to tell you the buses will be here in about an hour. I'd like everyone to meet at the flagpole in thirty minutes so I can go over a few things."

"I'll make sure everyone is ready."

"I know you will." He moved to leave, then paused. "And then maybe, once all of this is over, we can try that kissing thing again." His eyebrows waggled before he turned and continued on to the next cabin.

Blythe's insides fluttered as she made her way back inside. Had that really just happened? Had Daniel actually kissed her, or had she dreamed it?

No, he had definitely kissed her. Though the girls probably thought she'd gotten in trouble for coming down on them.

Back in the cabin, Carnie, the girl with the scarf, approached her as she entered. "I'm sorry for being a jerk." One slight shoulder lifted. "I guess you really do understand. I mean, being that you had cancer and got dumped on by that camp."

"I do, Carnie. And I hope when you look back on your camp experience here that it'll be the fun times you remember, not having to leave early because of something out of our control."

"Where are they taking us, anyway?"

"To the school in Ouray. Which reminds me." She stepped back, cupping her hands around her mouth so everyone could hear her. "Everyone needs to be at the flagpole in thirty minutes."

Chapter Twelve

Daniel did not want to do this. He hated even the thought of disappointing these kids by taking them away from camp. A camp they had been looking forward to, where they were having fun and getting to partake in adventures they might never get to have again.

But thanks to that wildfire, he didn't have a choice.

Standing beside the flagpole, he stared out over the group of teens gathered on the grass around him, their bags at their feet, their eyes on him. Two school buses had already pulled in and rumbled in the distance, waiting to transport them to Ouray. Meaning he'd better go ahead and say what he needed to say so they could be on their way and out of this smoke that seemed to be growing even thicker.

"All right, gang. I'm really sorry, but there's nothing we can do about the weather, so let's consider this another part of the adventure, all right? I mean, just think about it. We'll have the whole school to ourselves with *no* teachers. I don't know about you, but when I was your age, that would have been a dream come true."

That garnered a round of cheers.

"I need all of you to stay with your companions, so we can make sure everyone is accounted for. Okay?"

"Yes, sir." The group responded collectively, though not necessarily enthusiastically.

"Good deal. You can start boarding now. If you need help with your bags, just ask any staff member for assistance."

As the kids started for the buses, Blythe came alongside him. "Good job. You always manage to put a positive spin on things."

At least he had somebody fooled. Because he certainly wasn't feeling very positive. "I can't let these kids down." Unfortunately, he already had.

Turning away, he headed for his SUV.

While companions rode on the buses with the kids, Daniel and most of the staff drove their own vehicles. Alone in his SUV, away from the chaos of the evacuation, the weight of the situation grew heavy.

"God, I don't understand." Daniel hadn't been able to pull off two weeks of camp. How would he be able to even think about expanding to four or six weeks the next year? His plans, his dream, seemed to be falling apart. "Why, God?"

He'd been so certain about Camp Sneffels. Everything had lined up perfectly, from the camp itself to the funding, the renovations and building…and for what? A measly eleven days.

Daniel had failed. And disheartened a lot of kids in the process.

Trust.

His mother's favorite word had been engrained in him since he was old enough to know what it meant.

Continuing down the highway, he eyed the mountaintops in the distance.

Trust usually wasn't an issue for Daniel. Some might call it blind faith. Pressing on with what he knew to be right, without knowing what lay ahead. So, what was his problem now?

Because he wanted so badly for the camp to be a success and for the kids to be happy.

Trust in the Lord with all thine heart; and lean not unto thine own understanding. The verse from Proverbs played across his heart, the way it had so many times before.

Daniel let go a frustrated sigh. Today he'd been presented with an opportunity to trust. And, so far, his answer had been a big fat no.

He slowed at the Ouray City Limit sign. *Forgive me, God. I may not understand, but I can choose to trust. So, from this moment on, that's what I'm going to do.* Because if he lost hope, the kids would, too. And he couldn't allow that to happen.

He pulled up to the school before the buses and hurried inside for a quick look at the arrangements. They'd likely have cots set up, maybe some tables and chairs.

Tugging open the gymnasium door, he saw a handful of people inside, scurrying back and forth, doing who knew what. Then he did a double take.

Brown paper gift bags with green tissue paper sticking out lined a table to the right of the door.

"Daniel."

He turned as two of his sisters-in-law, Carly, Andrew's wife, and Lily, Noah's wife, made their way toward him.

"Ladies," he acknowledged with a nod. "What are these?" He pointed to the bags.

"Just a few things we thought the kids might need." Carly grinned.

"You know they're bringing their stuff with them?"

"Doesn't matter." Lily tucked her reddish-blond hair behind her ear. "One can never have enough toothbrushes, toothpaste, socks—"

"Socks?" Color him confused.

"To keep their feet warm." Lily rested a hand on her growing belly. Come October, Daniel was going to be an uncle again. Just in time for Noah and Lily's first wedding anniversary.

"There's also a small bottle of water and some snacks," added Carly.

"Speaking of snacks…" Lily motioned for Daniel to follow them to one side of the gym where two tables were overflowing with homemade cookies and brownies, chips, snack mixes and granola bars. "People have been dropping off stuff since we got here three hours ago."

He couldn't help laughing. "You did tell them the kids likely wouldn't be here for more than twenty-four hours, if that?"

"Yes," Carly nodded. "But you know how this town is, Daniel. If they see a need, they're going to meet it in a big way. We can always hold some of it back for tonight's campfire, though."

"Campfire?" He eyed Carly. "You know we're under a burn ban."

Both women seemed to get a good chuckle out of that.

"Not a real one, silly." Lily led him to one end of

the bleachers. "We borrowed this old washtub from the ranch."

"That was my grandmother's." Except he'd never seen it lined with rocks and stacked with wood with yellow and orange tissue paper shoved in between.

"When you're ready for the campfire effect," Lily stooped, her hand reaching for a small box, "you simply turn it on." Tiny LED lights glowed beneath the tissue paper, creating a glow similar to that of a campfire.

"Battery operated?" He helped Lily to her feet.

"That's right. So, it's ready whenever you are."

He glanced around the typically nondescript space that was now filled with an outpouring of love. "I can't believe you two were able to do all of this on such short notice. The goody bags, the campfire…" He looked from one blond to the other. "I definitely underestimated your creativity."

"Since all of you will be in here together, we thought the campfire might be a nice way for everyone to reflect on their camp experience as you close things out."

A lump formed in his throat. While he was busy second-guessing God, his sisters-in-law and the entire community had been working hard on behalf of his campers.

"Oh, and there's one more thing we have to tell you." Lily's grin moved from him to Carly, who appeared about ready to bounce right out of her shoes.

"Since parents aren't picking up the kids until tomorrow, we got in touch with the people who run the hot springs pool. All of the campers, volunteers and staff are welcome tonight, free of charge."

Daniel had to look away then as tears pricked at his eyes. Not only was he overwhelmed with the outpouring of support, he felt so unworthy. *God, forgive me for doubting.*

Collecting himself, he faced Carly and Lily once again. "The kids are going to love that. Thank you. You two have taken what could have been an uber downer, boring experience for the kids and turned it into something I never could have imagined. Thank you." He held his arms wide then, motioning both of them to bring it in for a group hug.

"And just for the record, my brothers have really good taste in women."

By three o'clock the following day, all of the campers had been picked up, the gymnasium had been returned to its original state and volunteers and staff were on their way back to Camp Sneffels. Yet while most of the companions rode the bus, Blythe hadn't been able to say no when Daniel asked her if she wanted to ride with him. With all of the frenzy of the past twenty-four hours, they hadn't had much opportunity to talk.

"I hate to admit this—" she eyed him across the center console of his SUV "—because you'll probably chastise me for my lack of faith, but I was afraid the evacuation and being at the school was going to be a huge letdown for everyone. Especially the kids. But what those people pulled off—your sisters-in-law, the town—was truly amazing. Those kids were so stoked over the hot springs, I don't think they even missed the camp."

Both hands on the steering wheel, Daniel stared straight ahead as the corners of his mouth tipped upward. "I think you're right. Except for the part about me chastising you. That would make me rather hypo-critical."

"Hypocritical?"

His blue eyes briefly darted her way before return-ing to the road. "My faith faltered, too. That is, until I remembered that I'm not in control. I was really hum-bled and convicted when I walked into that gym. My selfish desires would have robbed all those folks of a huge blessing."

Blythe simply stared at him, realizing that fighting these feelings growing inside of her was becoming more difficult by the day. Daniel was everything she'd ever wanted in a man and more. Not only did he have great faith, he was sincere, caring, noble... Oh, and incred-ibly handsome. The kind of man she'd once dreamed of marrying and spending the rest of her life with. A dream that had died long ago, never to be revived. Until now.

Except you live in Denver and Daniel lives in Ouray.

She should have known he was too good to be true.

Clearing her throat, she said, "God sure knows how to do things in a big way."

Daniel chuckled as he turned at the light in Ridgway. "He certainly does."

"So, what do we do now?" she asked. "I mean, when we get back to camp."

"Well, the original plan would have allowed volun-teers to head home Saturday night or Sunday. Some have to be back to work on Monday." He shrugged. "So, I guess I'll let them leave whenever they like. The staff and I will be meeting tomorrow to go over things to see what worked, what didn't and any changes we'd like to see."

"Could I be a part of that?" She was discovering that

she really liked being involved in the planning and operation of the camp.

Smiling, he said, "I'd actually like that very much, especially since you're apt to have some insight into both campers and companions." His grip on the steering wheel relaxed. "I think everyone might prefer to just chill tonight, though."

Having talked with many of her fellow companions, she knew most of them planned to hang around tonight, too, and head out in the morning when they were fresh. That had her recalling the fun of their team-building exercises and how they'd all gotten to know one another since then. "I have a thought."

His grin tangled her insides.

"What if you had a going away party tonight? They are volunteers, after all. It would be a nice way to let them know how much you appreciate them. Besides, it would be kind of a last hurrah for us adults. A chance to say our goodbyes."

"You're just full of good ideas today, aren't you?"

Heat crept into her cheeks. It surprised her how much she'd enjoyed planning all these parties and events. Made her wonder if she'd missed her calling. "I try."

"How would you suggest I execute something like that?"

She lifted a shoulder. "We had parties in the chow hall for the kids. Why not for the adults?"

He eased off the highway onto the dirt road that wound its way up to the camp. "Do you think Juanita would mind? I mean, I know she's making dinner for tonight, and it's kind of short notice to throw in a party."

Juanita had brought the enchiladas she'd prepared early yesterday to the school for last night's dinner, then whipped up some tasty breakfast tacos in the school's kitchen this morning.

"Not necessarily. We never touched any of the party snacks she'd planned for yesterday afternoon because we had to leave. So, we know she's got nacho stuff and popcorn."

"And probably a whole lot more, if I know her." He nodded. "I like that."

"Of course you do. We all do. Because when it comes to junk food, we're all just big kids."

"You got that right."

"Why don't we go talk to her first and let her know what the plans are?" Blythe pulled out her phone. "In the meantime, I'll text Teri and tell her to let everyone know we're planning a going away party for tonight."

"Sounds good." He wound around the final bend that approached the camp office. "Hey, maybe we could come up with some kind of award for everyone. You know, silly awards, like the Peacock Award for the biggest show-off."

"Levi. Especially when Teri's around."

"Or the Fourth and Long Award for the person most likely to come through in a clutch."

"Teri."

"Or you."

"Me?" Brow lifted, she faced him. "Hardly."

He brought his SUV to a stop in front of the office and killed the engine. "Do you know how many times you've come through for me since you got here? You're one of those people I know I can count on. Just look at what we're doing right now. Collaborating on this impromptu party." His blue eyes bored into her, doing a real number on her heart rate.

"It wouldn't be polite for me to suggest it and then not be willing to help."

He smoothed the back of his hand over her cheek. "I really like that you suggested it."

Fortunately, he opened his door and stepped out of the vehicle then. Giving her a moment to rein in the crazy thoughts his touch ignited.

When she emerged a few moments later, she noticed a haze still hung in the air, though the smoke smell wasn't as noticeable as yesterday.

"Look at this." Daniel pointed to the golf cart beside the office.

Rounding his SUV, she saw a layer of ash now coated the once shiny green paint.

Eyes wide, she looked up at him. "I'm glad we got the kids out of here when we did."

"Me, too." He scanned the rest of area before sending her a killer smile. "I'm going to run over to the chow hall and talk to Juanita. You're welcome to join me."

"Sure." She fell in step beside him, fully aware that spending time with Daniel was like playing with fire and she knew her heart would likely be burned. However, until a few weeks ago, she'd walked her whole life on the safe side of the street. Now that she'd crossed over to where all the fun was, not to mention one really cute camp director, she wasn't sure how she'd feel about going back.

Chapter Thirteen

Blythe couldn't believe they'd done it again. Pulled off another wildly successful party with little time to prepare.

Last night's event had gone on until nearly midnight. Seemed their impromptu farewell party was just what everyone needed after camp had come to a premature end. It gave volunteers an opportunity to talk about their experiences and share how they'd been impacted with those who would understand best. Memories had definitely been made in these past two weeks. Happy memories, touching moments, even a few tearjerkers.

In the end, everyone agreed that their experience at Camp Sneffels was one they would cherish for the rest of their lives, and many were already prepared to sign up for next year. Including Blythe. Especially after the staff meeting she'd just come from.

The staff had been huddled in the chow hall since ten o'clock this morning, comparing notes, discussing what worked and what hadn't, and suggesting things they'd like to add for next year. Like a climbing wall and white-water rafting trips for the older kids.

Now, as the midafternoon sun inched across the sky, Blythe emerged from the chow hall into the blessedly haze-free air. According to Daniel's brother Matt, fire-fighters had gained control of the fire during the wee hours of the morning. They just prayed that the winds wouldn't kick up again and reignite the blaze.

With the staff meeting behind her, she was on a mission. Daniel had invited her to his father's wedding tomorrow night, and she didn't have anything appropriate to wear. Which meant it was time to go shopping.

"Once again, you offered up some stellar ideas, Blythe."

She'd been so lost in her thoughts, she hadn't even realized Daniel was beside her. His praise had her bordering on giddy. Throw in the fact that she was going to be his date, and the sixteen-year-old girl inside of her was ready to squeal. Okay, so was the twenty-eight-year-old woman. But that would definitely be inappropriate.

Moving across the grass in the direction of her cabin, she glimpsed the handsome camp director to her left. "I wasn't the only one. You've assembled a good team, Daniel."

"I won't argue with you there. However, I like that you come at things from a different perspective. Did you know you have a real knack for planning?"

She couldn't help laughing. "That's because I've done it all of my adult life. Comes with that desire to play things safe. So, it's a nice switch to be able to throw out some spontaneous ideas."

"In that case, I don't suppose I could talk you into being a permanent part of my team?"

She stopped then. So did he. Peering up into his blue eyes, she could have said yes in a heartbeat. That was, if she'd thought Daniel meant what he said. But he was simply being kind. Besides, in two days, she'd be loading up her car and heading back to Denver.

"I think you're on your way to having a really great camp next year."

His expression went flat, his eyes widened. "Does that mean the camp will receive funding from the Ridley Foundation?"

He looked so stunned she couldn't help smiling. "The board will have the final say, but that will be my recommendation, yes."

His grin was a slow one, eventually hitting max wattage. "I—" Looking every bit the camp director in his cargo shorts and green Camp Sneffels polo, he shoved his fingers through his hair. "I don't know what to say."

"How about nothing? At least, not yet. Not until we hear what the board has to say."

He nodded repeatedly. "Yes, you are absolutely right." Hands perched low on his hips, he sucked in a breath of smoke-free air. "Where are you headed?"

"To my cabin to change." Something that was going to be really strange now that she was the only person left in that big cabin. "And then I'm going to Montrose."

His smile faded. Almost as though he was disappointed. "Why?"

"Because I need a dress for the wedding."

"Oh." Suddenly his eyes sparked to life again, as though he'd been struck with inspiration. "What about those sundresses you mentioned at All Geared Up?"

"They're too casual for a wedding. I don't suppose there's a dress shop in Ouray?"

"There's the Paisley Elk." He thoughtfully rubbed the stubble on his chin. "However, I might have a better idea." He pulled his phone from his pocket and scrolled through the screen. "What size do you wear?"

A breeze rustled through the leaves overhead as her arms instinctively crossed over her chest. "I can't believe you just asked me that."

"I have a good reason." He set the phone to his ear.

She continued to watch him. The man was up to something. "Who are you calling?"

"Lily."

"Your sister-in-law?"

"Yes. You two look like you're about the same size. Well, when she's not pregnant, that is. And until last fall, she was a prominent member of Denver society."

"She—?" Lily? Denver society? She felt her eyes go wide. "Wait. Lily Davis?"

"That's the one. Or was, anyway. Now she's Lily Stephens."

No wonder she'd looked familiar. There had been a time when the woman was all over Denver television and the society pages. According to people who knew her, some of whom Blythe had run into at Ridley Foundation functions, she was very sweet, which was the same impression Blythe had gotten yesterday. And she was married to Daniel's cowboy brother. Boy, talk about a change in lifestyle.

"Lily. Hey, it's Daniel."

Blythe lowered her arms, watching and waiting.

"Not too much at the moment. Hey, Blythe needs a dress for Dad's wedding tomorrow. Do you suppose you could help her out?"

He was silent for a long moment.

"Great. I'll let her know. Thanks, Lily."

Shoving the phone back into his pocket, he sent

Blythe a satisfied smile. "She says she's got an entire closetful of dresses at the ranch house and she'd be happy to meet us there. Except we need to make it soon. She promised Hillary's daughter, Celeste, she'd help decorate Granny's Kitchen for the rehearsal dinner."

"Oh, that's right. I guess they would be having that tonight. I hate to impose on her, then."

"You're not imposing, I promise. And maybe, after you choose a dress, we could swing by All Geared Up so you can pick up those sundresses before we head over to the church."

"What's at the church?"

"The wedding rehearsal. Then they're doing a private dinner at the restaurant. Originally, I wasn't going to be able to attend. But now that the campers are gone…" He moved closer, reaching for her hand. "Care to join me?"

Her insides bubbled with more happiness than she'd known in a long time. Did she dare to dream? Or was she simply setting herself up for heartbreak?

If there was one thing she'd learned these past couple of weeks, it was that life was much more fun when there was a little risk involved. Like Daniel said, life was an adventure.

"I think that sounds like a pretty fun way to spend an evening. I get a dress for the wedding, plus the sundresses *and* I get to spend time with you and your family."

The smile he sent her was like the sun's rays, warming her through and through. "Guess we'd better get going then."

"Just let me grab some shoes that'll go with one of those sundresses, and I'll be ready."

"Why do they need to go with the sundress?"

"Because that's what I'm planning to wear tonight, silly." Though she probably ought to change, just in case they were gone. The thought had her giving Daniel a quick once-over. "And unless you plan to wear your uniform to tonight's event, you might want to consider changing, too."

Daniel grew nauseous every time he thought about Blythe leaving. He had to find a way to make the most of these last few days they had together. To make them so memorable, Blythe couldn't wait to come back. Or better yet, make her want to stay. And his father's wedding tomorrow, not to mention tonight's rehearsal, might be just the ticket.

Since she didn't have to run off to Montrose for a dress, he'd get to spend the entire evening with her. Thanks to Lily. He hoped they were meeting with success. Blythe, Hillary, Lily and Lily's eight-year-old daughter, Piper, had been inside the house for at least thirty minutes, while he remained outside with his father, filling him in on things that had transpired at the camp these past two weeks.

Yet as the late afternoon sun blazed overhead, making Daniel grateful they were in the shade, the conversation took a turn.

Sitting at the first of two picnic tables atop the wooden deck that spanned one end of the single-story cedar ranch house, Dad wore that grin Daniel had become accustomed to seeing as the man played matchmaker for each of his brothers over the past couple of years.

"So, she's coming to the wedding with you, is she?" The glimmer in the old man's dark eyes was hard to miss.

"All right, Dad, I'm going to cut to the chase. Yes, I like Blythe. Does she like me? I have no idea."

Back against the tabletop, his father crossed his booted feet at the ankles. "She agreed to be your date, didn't she?"

That, at least, gave Daniel hope. "Yeah. However, she lives in Denver and will be going back very soon."

One dark brow lifted. "How soon?"

"Sunday." He eyed the barn across the way and the cattle searching the drought-stricken pasture beyond for food. "But I'm going to do my best to talk her into coming back next weekend for the Fourth."

"And after that?"

"I don't know." He shrugged. "We'll just have to see what God has planned."

"Don't approach that so lightly, son. Because He certainly defeated some odds to work things out for your brothers." The man straightened, resting his forearms on his denim-clad thighs. "They all faced potential separation just like you're talking about. And in each case, God brought about a change in plans."

The door to the mudroom opened then, and a smiling Hillary emerged. The attractive blonde Daniel and his brothers had grown to love over the past two years looked as though she'd just stepped from the pages of a magazine in her tailored white slacks, a colorful print blouse and silver sandals that revealed bright pink toenails.

"How's it going in there?" Daniel watched her as she moved toward them.

"Blythe has narrowed things down to a couple of options." Hillary eased beside him. "She's a lovely young woman, Daniel. I hope you asked her to join us for the rehearsal and dinner."

"Yeah, since things changed up at camp, I went ahead and extended the invitation. I hope you don't mind."

"Mind? Your father and I would be disappointed if the two of you weren't there. Celeste will have more than enough food." Hillary's daughter owned Granny's Kitchen but had closed the restaurant for the night so they could hold the dinner there.

He found himself smiling. "All right, then. We'll definitely be there."

The back door opened again, and Piper bounded outside, her blonder-than-blond ponytail swaying back and forth, while her mother and Blythe followed.

Standing, Daniel said, "Did you meet with success?"

"Wait till you see, Uncle Daniel." Piper peered up at him. "Blythe looks *bea-utiful*." She twirled then, as if adding an exclamation point to her statement.

"I have to say…" A hanger dangled from Blythe's fingers, a gray plastic sheath concealing her selection. "That was the toughest shopping I've ever done. Lily has so many gorgeous dresses."

"I'm glad I was able to help." His sister-in-law gave Blythe a quick one-armed hug. "And just for the record, that dress looks a thousand times better on you than it ever did on me."

"I doubt that," said Blythe. "But thank you so much. I promise to take good care of it."

Daniel inched toward the two, curious as to what was hidden underneath the hanger's covering. "If you still want to stop by All Geared Up for those sundresses, we should probably get a move on."

Her hazel eyes skimmed his attire, followed by an approving smile. "You changed."

"Right about the time you ladies started discussing

dresses." He hadn't taken any of his Sunday clothes to the camp, so he'd had to wait until they were here to don his chinos and a blue polo.

"You're right, though. I do need to make my shopping trip quick because I'm going to help Lily and your other sisters-in-law decorate for the dinner."

"Oh?" His tone lingered somewhere between confusion and disappointment. How were they supposed to be together if she was doing that?

His father stood and slapped him on the back. "Looks like you'll have to join me and your brothers over at Matt's."

While that was fine, Daniel would much rather have been with Blythe.

"Yes, the men will be playing while we women are working," said Hillary.

"What are you talkin' about, woman?" Dad frowned at his bride-to-be. "We're the ones doing the babysitting."

"Pft." Hillary waved a hand through the air. "Clint Stephens, you love nothing more than being with those grandkids."

"Now that is a fact." Pausing beside her father-in-law, Lily aimed a finger in his direction. "And don't you dare try to deny it." She winked then. "Come on, Piper. We have work to do."

The duo continued down the steps toward a luxury SUV.

"See you ladies shortly." Lily waved before disappearing into her vehicle.

Blythe eyed Daniel. "We need to run, too."

They loaded into his SUV and started down the road, with the river on one side and a wall of red sandstone to their left.

"Tell you what." She twisted to face him. "Since the restaurant is less than a block from the store, why don't you just drop me off? That way you have more time to hang out with your brothers."

While he appreciated her thoughtfulness, he groaned inside, his grip tightening on the steering wheel. "I'd rather hang out with you." Had he really just admitted that out loud?

The slow smile that teased her pretty pink lips said he had. "It's only for a little while. Besides, helping will make me feel better about borrowing Lily's dress."

"In that case, I will try to manage." He rolled up Main Street, looking for a parking space. Given that it was a Friday evening, the town was bustling with people. "We still have tomorrow to go on an adventure."

"Adventure?" Anticipation sparked in her pretty eyes. "What do you have in mind?"

He angled into a spot, shifted into Park and looked her way. "That's for me to know and you to find out."

Her giggle wrapped around his heart and refused to let go. "Glad to see you decided to be mature about this."

"You ought to know by now that I'm just a kid at heart."

"In that case, you're the handsomest kid ever."

Over the center console, their eyes locked, and for a moment, time seemed to stand still. Cars and passersby faded in the distance. He longed to taste her lips again. But then they might never make it to the wedding rehearsal.

Glancing at the people streaming in and out of the store, he said, "Guess you'd better get going."

"Okay." She reached for the door handle. "See you shortly?"

"*That* you can count on."

Chapter Fourteen

By the next morning, Blythe knew beyond a shadow of a doubt that her feelings for Daniel had drifted beyond friendship. Something new and different had unfolded between them last night. Something she couldn't name, yet she'd felt it all the way down to her toes.

Maybe it was being with his family, watching the dynamics and seeing the genuine love they had for one another. Quite different from her family where her mother's conditional love so often turned family gatherings into arguments.

So-called bad choices, including Jenna's marriage, had caused their mother to disown Blythe's sister. Blythe's father kowtowed to the woman's every whim, instead of being the leader God had called him to be. And Blythe had tried in vain to be the glue that held their family together.

Then her parents moved to Tucson, in part because her mother had decided she couldn't tolerate winter anymore, despite having lived her entire life in Colorado. At first, Blythe had contemplated following them. Then she realized her stress level had dropped considerably after her parents were gone. She was able to enjoy her time with Jenna and her family instead of feeling guilty about it.

With their parents out of the picture, Blythe and Jenna forged a new family. One where they accepted each other for who they were, not who they thought they should be. Holidays became more festive. Birthdays a blessing. And now that they were so far away, her parents seem happier, too. Perhaps ignorance really was bliss.

Blythe liked Daniel's family. But that wasn't what had caused her shift. No, it was much simpler than that. It was the way Daniel made her feel when she was with him. Special, like no one and nothing else mattered.

Like last night when they'd returned to camp. Daniel had insisted they move her things back to the small cabin where she'd be closer to him and the rest of the staff. To the cabin that should have been his. His protectiveness had warmed her heart as much as it flooded her with relief. Just the thought of being alone in that big cabin she'd shared with Chloe, Evie, Teri and the other girls, away from everyone else, had her feeling a little uneasy.

Regardless of what had caused her change in perspective, she'd given herself over to the possibilities that lay ahead. And given that she and Daniel were spending all of Saturday together, those possibilities seemed endless.

She'd awakened early this morning, unable to sleep because of all the anticipation tumbling around inside of her. *We still have tomorrow to go on an adventure*, he'd said. Well, tomorrow had arrived, and she couldn't wait to see what he had in store.

So she promptly gathered up her things once again, loaded them into her car and moved them all to Ouray where she'd remain until tomorrow. Since the wedding and cleanup were likely to run late and it would be inappropriate for Blythe to stay alone with Daniel at the ranch house, Carly had offered Blythe a room at her bed and breakfast. And while Blythe had offered to pay for the room, Carly wanted nothing to do with that.

Now she stood on the expansive front porch of Granger House Inn, Carly's gorgeous Victorian B and B, watching Daniel move up the steps just after ten. He was dressed pretty much the same way he'd been every day at Camp Sneffels—cargo shorts and T-shirt—except this shirt was gray with the words Live Adventurously scrawled across the front.

Grinning, he said, "Ready for an adventure?"

Only weeks ago, she would have scoffed at the words. Today, the invitation had her eager to follow him anywhere.

"I thought you'd never ask."

They piled into his SUV and headed south of town on the Million Dollar Highway, a road she'd heard of but never actually been on. It didn't take long to understand why this stretch of highway was so notorious. The roadway snaked its way along the sides of the mountains, hugging a wall of rock on one side as sheer drop-offs threatened on the other. And every time it appeared they were in the clear, another hairpin turn was waiting just ahead.

They'd driven about twenty minutes when Daniel eased off the highway onto a narrow road. Only a few hundred yards in, they were met with an orange and white barricade.

"Uh-oh." Looking across the center console, she noted Daniel's mischievous smile. "What are you up to?"

"I'll be right back." With that, he hopped out of the vehicle, marched along the gravel until he came to the barrier, then promptly moved it out of their path before returning to the SUV.

"Daniel Stephens—" she scolded as he reclaimed the driver's seat "—that barricade was there for a reason, you know."

"Yes, it was. For a very good reason." Grinning, he moved the vehicle beyond the barrier.

Drawing her brows together, she waited for him to continue.

"We put it there to keep Ouray's many visitors out." With that, he again shifted into Park and went to return the barricade to its original spot. When he returned, he said, "Hey, we love our guests, but we locals still like to keep a few secrets." He rolled down the windows and put the vehicle into four-wheel drive before continuing up the rocky slope.

Towering conifers stretched to their left and right, occasionally allowing them a glimpse of nearby peaks. They moved at almost a crawl as the SUV rocked back and forth. The narrow road curved and Blythe glimpsed something in the woods.

"What is that?"

Daniel stopped the vehicle. "Just some old mining equipment." He opened his door. "Come on, let's check it out."

She hurried to join him as he moved limbs out of the way and motioned for her to go ahead.

Easing into the woods, she studied the dilapidated

structure. A large wooden wheel still clung to an iron shaft on a wooden tower, while old boards lay haphazardly atop what might have been a platform. "Any idea what it was used for?" Tugging her phone from the back pocket of her shorts, she snapped a few pictures.

"I suspect it was part of a tram that they would use to carry the buckets of ore down the mountain."

"Gold?"

"Or silver. Both had their heyday in the area."

"That is so cool." She took a couple more shots. "Okay, I'm ready."

Back in the SUV, they continued their journey deeper into the forest, farther up the mountain.

"It's a little early for wildflowers." Daniel held tight to the steering wheel. "And given our drought, things aren't as green as usual, but I think we might find a hidden gem that overcomes the obstacles."

Suddenly, she was even more excited about what lay ahead. She'd never gone into the mountains like this before, yet Daniel seemed to know exactly where they were headed.

"Right around this bend…" he continued.

The dust that had accompanied their journey to that point seemed to fade. A fresh fragrance filled the air, something crisp and earthy. And the sound of rushing water touched her ears.

"Is that a stream I hear?"

Daniel remained silent as they completed their turn. Moments later, she saw something so glorious, it took her breath away.

Straight ahead, a stream spilled down the mountain in a narrow strip, splashing over jagged rocks and fallen limbs while brilliant green foliage sprang from its rocky banks. Trees shaded one side as the sun highlighted a spray of white flowers on the other.

Stepping out of the vehicle, she took picture after picture, trying in vain to capture the beauty. When she finally found her voice, she moved beside Daniel. "This is so pretty. How did you ever find it?"

"It's amazing what you encounter when you venture off the beaten path." Obviously a nod to her rather safe lifestyle.

Heat crept into her cheeks as she peered up into his blue eyes. "Something I'm learning to do."

"And thanks to that barricade, we've probably got the place to ourselves." He motioned around them.

"You know, aside from your office or your car, this is about the only place we have been alone."

"Then I guess we should make the most of it. Grab a bite to eat, take a little hike…"

She gazed around at their surroundings. "And what do you propose we eat? Wild berries?"

"No, I brought lunch." Returning to the SUV, he reached through the open window of the driver's side back door and pulled out a bag and a blanket. "Care to join me?" He moved to a grassy area beside the water where the sun speckled through the trees and handed her the bag before spreading the blanket on the ground.

"Of course, I'll join you." Crossing her ankles, she lowered herself onto the Southwestern-style blanket, taking in the crystal waters, blue sky and alpine forest. "It'll give me a chance to absorb all of this untouched beauty."

Sitting on the other end of the blanket, he pulled two wrapped sandwiches from the bag. "Here you go." He handed one to her. "Ranch house special."

She wasn't sure what a ranch house special was, but she accepted it anyway, eager to find out. "Thank you."

Surrounded by the sounds of bubbling water and bird songs, she removed the sandwich from the bag. And though she hadn't had white bread in years, she took a bite.

"Mmm!" Still chewing, she stared at the roast beef in surprise. "This is amazing." While the bread lulled her into a comforting cocoon, the tang of horseradish awakened her senses. So, this was how cattle ranchers did beef. Nice!

Daniel puffed out a laugh. "Let me guess, you've never had a homemade roast beef sandwich, have you?"

"Don't be silly. Of course, I have." Picking off a chunk of beef, she popped it into her mouth, savoring the flavor while she stared at the moving water. "Except the shaved meat came out of a package and it was on nine-grain bread."

His handsome face contorted. "Sounds kind of boring to me."

She released a sigh before meeting his sparkling blue gaze. "It was."

Taking a bite of his own sandwich, he stretched his long legs across the blanket. "So you enjoyed your time with my sisters-in-law, huh?"

She swallowed another bite. "Yes, I really did. They welcomed me with open arms."

"Any observations?"

"You mean, other than the fact that they're prolific?" Seemed everyone either had a baby or was pregnant.

He leaned on one elbow. "Yeah, kind of funny how it was just us guys for years and then suddenly everyone's getting married and having kids." He stared at her then. "Maybe one day I can join their ranks. Perhaps sooner than I thought."

His words wound through her being, warming her heart and terrifying her at the same time.

"Does that mean you want kids?"

He sat up then. "Absolutely."

Her appetite waned. She shouldn't have asked such a stupid question. Of course Daniel wanted kids. She'd seen the way he was at camp, how good he was with the campers, no matter what their age.

Except Blythe might not be able to give Daniel the family he longed for. Making her wonder why she'd given herself over to this relationship in the first place. Because the only thing she was likely to come away with was a giant hole in her heart.

Sitting in the sanctuary of Restoration Fellowship that night with Blythe at his side, Daniel was blown away by how amazing God truly was.

Four years ago, his family had been rocked by his mother's death. Dad had been lost without the woman who'd been the sun of his solar system, and Daniel and his brothers hadn't fared much better. Mama had been their guiding light for their entire lives, and suddenly she was gone, leaving them floundering in a sea of heartache.

Then, slowly but surely, things began to change. Daniel embarked on a venture inspired by his mother, one that gave his life new meaning. And one by one his brothers had found love, gotten married and started families. Now, as he watched Dad pledge his life and love to Hillary, Daniel couldn't help wondering if he'd found the woman God had intended for him.

Holding tight to Blythe's hand, he smiled her way. He'd enjoyed watching her change and grow in the two weeks since they'd met. He liked her spirit. The way she wasn't afraid to step up and help, whether it was becoming a camp companion, planning a party or caring for a sick child. But she was vulnerable, too. Something she didn't want others to see, yet he kind of liked it.

Yes, the woman at his side seemed to become more irresistible with each passing day. And the way she looked tonight in that ultrafeminine ocean-blue dress solidified his desire to make a long-distance relationship work. He just wished he knew why she'd seemed so nervous when he picked her up.

"The couple has chosen to write their own vows," Pastor Dan announced to the guests that were packed into the small sanctuary.

Daniel tucked his thoughts away for the moment and concentrated on his father and the woman *he* loved.

Taking hold of his bride's hand, Dad looked more than a little nervous. "Hillary, I might not say it often enough, but I love you." The mere fact that the man was wearing a suit attested to that fact. "When you walked into my sad shell of a life, you were like a breath of fresh air. Or maybe a kick in the pants."

The entire congregation chuckled, and the old man grinned as his bride playfully swatted him.

"Whatever the case," he continued, "you made me feel alive again. Hillary, you're a trusted friend who's so pretty you make my heart turn cartwheels whenever we're together. Here, in front of all these people, I pledge my love to you, today and always. And I promise to do my best to make you every bit as happy as you've made me."

Daniel found himself blinking as the pastor turned things over to Hillary.

Wearing a knee-length satiny dress in what Blythe had called a champagne color, Hillary clutched his father's hand, her thumb moving back and forth over his knuckles.

"Clint..." Her voice broke. "You made me believe in love again. You're a living example of what unconditional love truly means. You have loved me even when I was at my worst. You healed my battered heart." Her voice cracked again, and her bottom lip quivered. "And gave me hope." She paused, dabbing a tissue to her eyes. Smiling, she regarded her intended. "Today, I give you my heart and my future. I love you, too, Clint Stephens, for the rest of my days."

"May I have the rings, please?" Pastor Dan looked to Noah first, who was serving as best man, then to Hillary's daughter and matron-of-honor, Celeste.

After a brief prayer, the pastor handed the first gold band to Daniel's father. "Place this on the ring finger of Hillary's left hand and repeat after me. I give you this ring as a symbol of my love, and with all that I am, I honor you, in the name of the Father, and of the Son and of the Holy Spirit."

With a trembling voice, Dad repeated the words.

By the time Hillary slid the ring onto his father's left hand, Daniel felt as though he had a boulder lodged in his throat. He never imagined this ceremony would be so emotional. He hadn't reacted like this at his brothers' weddings. Then again, this was Dad. The man who was supposed to spend forever with their mother. But God had other plans. This wedding was proof that God really could work *all* things together for good.

Finally, the pastor addressed the congregation. "Now that Hillary and Clint have given themselves to each other by solemn vows, with the joining of hands and the giving and receiving of rings, I pronounce that they are husband and wife, in the name of the Father, and the Son, and the Holy Spirit. Those whom God has joined together, let no one put asunder." The pastor then smiled at Daniel's father. "Clint, you may kiss your bride."

"'Bout time." The old man grinned, pulling his new wife to him.

Moments later, the entire church applauded as the happy couple made their way down the aisle.

When Daniel looked at Blythe, he noticed the unshed tears glistening in her pretty eyes.

"That was the sweetest wedding ever." She peered up at him, blinking.

Not as sweet as the one he was envisioning in his mind. Except he and Blythe had the starring roles in that version.

Easy, buddy. You're getting ahead of yourself.

Perhaps. But he was definitely going to talk to her about returning to Ouray for the town's annual Fourth of July celebration.

After photos, guests and family alike made their way to the ranch where a big white tent had been set up in the pasture behind the house for the reception. Since the high season was in full swing in Ouray, having the reception at the ranch seemed the logical choice. So Dad and Hillary had gone with a tent, the way Noah and Lily had for their wedding last October.

By the time they'd finished dinner, Daniel wondered if Blythe wasn't feeling a little overwhelmed. She'd been unusually quiet all evening. But with all of his family and almost half the town in attendance, it was understandable.

"Why don't we take a little walk?" He stood, pushed in his chair, then held a hand out to her.

She studied it a moment before taking hold.

Silently, they walked outside as the last rays of sunlight glowed behind the mountains that formed a backdrop for the ranch.

"Are you warm enough?" Temps fell off quickly once the sun went down and given that he was wearing a jacket and she was in a sleeveless dress…

"I'm fine." So she said, but the way she rubbed her arms had him removing his jacket and placing it over her shoulders anyway.

She sent him a knowing look.

"Your mouth says one thing, but your actions say another. I just don't want you to be uncomfortable."

Tugging the jacket around her, she said, "Thank you."

He shoved his hands into his pockets as they strolled toward the house. "July Fourth is just a little over a week away. I don't know if you've heard, but Ouray puts on quite a celebration."

"Oh?"

"No fireworks this year because of the drought, but they'll still have the parade and, of course, the fire hose fights."

"Fire hose fights?" Her curious gaze met his.

"You gotta see 'em to believe them." His steps slowed as they reached the deck. Facing her, he reached for her hand. "If you don't have plans already, I thought maybe you could come back, and we could go together."

Something akin to sadness filled her hazel eyes.

"Please don't do this, Daniel. I know we've had fun these past couple weeks and yes, I really enjoy spending time with you. But we both know that a long-distance relationship will never work."

"How can we know that when we haven't even tried?"

"Because it just won't."

He searched those beautiful eyes, looking for some clue as to why she was suddenly shutting down the possibility of a relationship. "In case you haven't noticed, there's something pretty special happening between us. Why would you not want to explore that?"

"Because it—because I—" Hugging herself, she turned away. "Because you want children, and I don't know if I'll be able to have them."

His mind had to work overtime to process what she was saying. "What do you mean you don't know?"

Still unwilling to face him, she tilted her head back and stared at the night sky. "The radiation. It left me with a fifty-fifty chance of conceiving. This afternoon, you said you wanted children. That tells me there's really no point in trying to pursue a relationship."

Daniel couldn't believe what he was hearing. She was pushing him away because she *might* not be able to have children? What kind of man did she think he was?

Moving in front of her, he said, "I definitely want children, Blythe."

Tears welled in her eyes.

"But as you experienced at camp, love knows no boundaries. Whether a child has your blood pumping through their veins isn't important. Love is all that matters. And I've been to enough places in this world to know that there are plenty of children just waiting for someone to love them." His gaze bored into hers, willing her to understand. "Blythe, I watched you with Chloe. You have the capability to love regardless of your connection to a child."

Tears spilled onto her cheeks, and he couldn't stop himself from hugging her. "Look, I don't know where this thing between us will lead, but don't *ever* think that whether or not you can give birth is an issue for me, because it's not." Taking a step back, he cupped her face in his hands, swiping her tears away with his thumbs. "And if some guy has ever made you feel like it was, then he's an idiot."

She puffed out a laugh. "Yes, he was an idiot." Surprisingly, she didn't make any effort to move, allowing him to get lost in those incredible eyes. Eyes he would miss terribly when she was gone.

Slowly, he lowered his head until their lips met. And while he wondered if she would kiss him back, he didn't wonder for long.

He wove his fingers into her soft hair and pulled her closer, longing to erase any doubt she might have about his feelings for her. She smelled like mountain flowers and sunshine.

Reluctantly, he broke the connection and rested his forehead against hers. "I love you, Blythe."

She pulled away, eyes wide as they searched his. Then the corners of her mouth tipped up as she said, "I think a Fourth of July in Ouray would be quite wonderful."

Chapter Fifteen

Blythe wasn't quite ready to let go of Ouray as she dressed for work Monday morning. Instead of her usual pants suit, she donned one of the sundresses she'd purchased at All Geared Up. Paired with a black sweater and some black heeled sandals, the black floral dress with the fitted bodice was the perfect compromise.

Her phone buzzed with a text message as she pulled into the Ridley Foundation's parking garage, though she didn't look at the screen until she'd parked in her assigned space. When she saw Daniel's name, a smile teased at her lips and her heart raced.

I'm back at the camp. It's not the same without you. Hope your first day back is a good one. Miss you.

Butterflies took flight in her belly. It had been less than twenty-four hours since they'd said goodbye, and she missed him terribly. While she'd been hesitant to say anything to Daniel, in her heart, she knew she loved him, too. And after everything he'd said to her Saturday night, that love had grown even more.

Now she had to endure five excruciating days before she could return to Ouray to see him. At least, she hoped Jack would give her the time off. Funny, it wasn't like her to make plans without carefully planning everything. But then, she wasn't the same person who'd checked out of this office almost three weeks ago.

Holding the phone with both hands, her thumbs quickly typed, Wish I was back at camp. Miss you, too.

After hitting Send, she grabbed her purse and computer bag and headed into the high-rise building. She took the elevator to the seventh floor, made her way through the stylishly appointed reception area and down the hall to her office where the only view was a piece of contemporary wall art that made no sense. The only thing it had going for it was that it was colorful. Still, it didn't hold any meaning.

She dropped her bags beside the L-shaped desk and retrieved her phone from her purse. One of those pictures she'd taken of the waterfall would look amazing in here. She pulled one up on her screen and held it toward the wall. Yes, all she had to do was get the image blown up and it would be perfect.

"Can I help you, miss?"

She whirled at the sound of Jack Hendershot's voice. "Hey, Jack."

"Blythe?" Continuing into the small office, he shook his head. "I've never seen you with your hair down before. And your clothes... I didn't recognize you."

Perhaps the changes she'd undergone in recent weeks were more significant than she thought. Granted, the hair was a biggie. Until recently, she'd always worn it in a bun. Very sleek and controlled. Just like her. Today, she'd simply washed it and let it air dry, leaving her with a nice wave she'd never known she had.

"Don't worry, Jack. It's just me."

"Apparently, camp suits you. And I'm not just talking about your tan. So how was it?" He plopped himself into the first of two chairs opposite the desk as she removed her laptop from its bag and set it atop her desk.

"As clichéd as it might sound, it was life changing."

"How so?" Jack leaned back and seemed to settle in for a long story.

"I learned to release control." *And I fell in love.* "Instead of trying to control the life God gave me, I discovered how to entrust Him with that life."

Her boss simply stared at her. "Daniel's good at driving that point home, isn't he?"

She eased into her faux leather desk chair. "He is. He caused me to look at my faith in ways I'd never done before." His love for Jesus was only one of the things she loved about him. "Which reminds me." She eased forward, resting her elbows on her glass and metal desk. "I was wondering if I could take off next week." Since the fourth was on Monday, it was only a four-day work week. "Or at least Tuesday."

Jack sent her a knowing grin. "I think half the staff is taking off next week."

She'd suspected as much.

"But," he continued, "that's likely the trend across the board, so sure. You can take the week."

"Really?" She practically leaped out of her chair with excitement. She chose to simply stand, instead.

"Really." The man who wasn't much younger than her father approached her. He knew Daniel. He knew her. He knew. He totally knew. "Ouray is a special place. Especially on the Fourth of July."

"I would have to agree." Though she'd say it was pretty special all year round. "Now, if you don't mind, I have to finish this report so the board will have it for their meeting tomorrow."

"Yes, ma'am." He playfully saluted her before turning to leave.

Blythe settled into her desk, trying to remember her old routine. One so rigid it would snap at the slightest deviation. Except she had deviated from the plotted course. Big-time. And honestly, she wouldn't have had it any other way.

Daniel had shown her how to live again. Not cautiously, not with calculation, but to really live. From where she sat, Daniel's heart was pure. His love for Jesus and positive outlook on life came through in everything he did. And his passion for helping kids live out their dreams was beyond measure. Daniel was the real deal. There was nothing phony about him. And she was drawn to him more than anyone she'd ever met.

Her phone vibrated beside her, and Daniel's name appeared on the screen. Picking it up, she tapped the button before placing the phone to her ear. "Hello."

"Just hearing your voice makes me feel better."

Her cheeks warmed. "What's going on at the camp? Anymore wildfires?"

"No, thank God. Levi and I are going to head over to Adventure Haven shortly to review some logistics and plot out where we might want to add that rock-climbing wall."

"Where are you now?"

"In my office." His office. Where many a late-night

chat had taken place. Where she'd confessed things she'd never told anyone else. Where she'd fallen in love with Daniel Stephens. "Though it's not near as much fun without you."

"I'll be there soon."

There was a long pause. Then, "You will?"

She couldn't help laughing. "Yes, Jack gave me next week off."

"And now I remember why I like him."

A beep sounded. She looked at her phone screen and saw Jenna's name. "Hey, Jenna's calling. Can I call you later?"

"Of course."

She quickly switched calls. At this rate, she'd never get her report done. "Hi, Jenna."

"Are you back?"

"I am. At least temporarily."

"Wait, wait, wait, what do you mean temporarily?"

She leaned back in her chair. "Well, I'm going back to Ouray this weekend for the Fourth."

"Why?"

"Because Daniel asked me."

There was a long pause. "Beach bum Daniel? The guy who was trying to schmooze you?"

Boy, did she need to set her sister straight. "No, Daniel the camp director. The one who encouraged me to take chances and taught me to live again."

"Oh, honey, you've got it bad. I think you need to join us for dinner tonight so we can talk."

"You mean I need to come by and spill while Adam puts the kids to bed?"

"Yeah, whatever."

"All right, *if* I can get this report done, I will come by tonight."

Her phone beeped again, and she peered at the screen. "I gotta go, Jenna. I'll update you later." She touched the button on the screen to switch calls. "Hello."

"Is this Blythe McDonald?" said the voice on the other end.

"Yes."

"This is Keisha from Denver Imaging. I was calling to remind you of your mammogram appointment, Wednesday at ten a.m."

Because of the radiation used to treat her lymphoma as a teen, her doctor had ordered routine screenings since she was twenty-five. Yet she'd completely forgotten.

Probably because, for the first time in her adult life, she was truly living. Actually enjoying life without having to worry about things like cancer screenings.

She promptly tugged her planner from her bag. She hadn't looked at it in over a week. Another testament to her drastic change.

Quickly thumbing to the appropriate page, she said, "Yes, Wednesday at ten. I will be there."

"No deodorants or lotions, please."

"That's right. I know the drill."

"All right then, Blythe. We will see you Wednesday."

Blythe ended the call, trying to ignore the panic that seemed to rise within her each and every time she got this call. She'd been cancer free for more than a dozen years now. There was no reason to worry. Especially now.

Closing her eyes, she declared her renewed stance. "God, I choose to trust You. No matter what, I will trust You."

* * *

Daniel stood in the silence of Camp Sneffels late Tuesday afternoon, realizing his work here was pretty much done for the moment. Sure, he'd still come up here regularly to check on things and see to the general upkeep of the place, but with no more campers, the real work wouldn't start again until next spring. That is, assuming the Ridley Foundation board approved the camp's funding.

He smiled as thoughts of Blythe played across his mind. Man, he missed her. And he hoped her input would have some influence on the board. Regardless of their decision, though, it was time for Daniel to find a place to live. Now that Dad and Hillary were married, living at the ranch house would be weird. Granted, they weren't your average newlyweds, but they were still newlyweds and would, no doubt, welcome a little privacy.

He glanced toward his office. He supposed he could continue to stay at the camp. At least for another week or so. Meaning he'd still need to find an apartment soon. Something that was going to be virtually impossible during the high season.

Ouray's population swelled during the summer months and not just because of its many visitors. The increase in guests meant a high demand for help from June to September. Hotels, restaurants, anything that had to do with tourism needed extra employees, making Ouray a huge draw for college students and anyone else looking to earn some extra money. Unfortunately, those people also needed places to live during those months. Leaving few options in either Ouray or Ridgway for someone like Daniel.

Looked like this was another opportunity to trust.

He climbed into his SUV. With his father gone, he'd been helping Noah put out feed for the cattle and make sure everything ran smoothly in his father's absence. Before he made it to the highway, though, his phone rang. And while he'd hoped to see Blythe's name on the screen, Jack Hendershot's name ran a close second.

His heart raced. *Lord, please let this be good news.*

Tapping the button, he placed the phone to his ear. "Hey, Jack. How's it going, buddy?"

"Quite well. I hear camp was a success."

"I think so." He stopped at the main road, looking left and right as cars whizzed by. "Though, not without a few problems."

"That's to be expected. Too bad that wildfire forced you to cut the second week short. From what I hear, though, the town really embraced the kids when you had to evacuate."

"They sure did." Suddenly warm, he adjusted the air vents. "And I think they were just as blessed by it as the kids."

"Community support is always beneficial."

"Agreed."

"Blythe was highly complimentary of the camp in her report. And I'm pleased to tell you that, because of her recommendation, the board has agreed to fund Camp Sneffels for not just one more year, but for five years."

Daniel's mouth fell open. "Five…" He shifted his vehicle into Park in case he passed out. "Five years? That's amazing."

"The board was quite impressed with both your passion for the kids and your love of adventure. They feel that five years will give you adequate opportunity to expand, not only in the number of camps you're able to host each year, but also Adventure Haven—which everyone was fascinated with. Any facilities, employees..."

As reality slowly began to sink in, tears stung Daniel's eyes. "This is truly unbelievable, Jack. I can't thank you enough. Your belief in me and this camp have been such an encouragement."

"I saw the joy you brought those patients when I went white water rafting with you in South America, and I knew you were the right man to pull this off."

Jack's use of the word *joy* almost had Daniel breaking down. That was the exact word his mother had used. *Bring joy into their lives the way you did mine.*

"I must say," Jack continued, "it appears you and Blythe hit it off rather well."

Heat crept up Daniel's neck. "It took a while, but yes, we did. She's a very special woman." Realizing what he'd said, his tender tone, he quickly added, "Though, I'm sure that had no influence on her report."

"Not on the report, no. Blythe is a professional. However, I'd say you had quite an influence on her."

While Daniel knew he'd helped her conquer her fears, he wasn't quite sure what Jack was getting at. "What do you mean?"

"Blythe's not the same person who left here three weeks ago. She's more relaxed, and she even looks different."

He curiously eyed the semi that rumbled past. "How so?"

"The entire time I've known Blythe, she's worn her hair in one of those slicked-back, tight buns. Now she's wearing her hair down in casual waves."

The way she'd done at the wedding. Daniel would never forget the feel or the smell of it.

"She's gone through quite a transformation, if you ask me."

"I'll be honest with you, Jack. I've never met anyone quite like her. A lot of the new ideas for the camp came from her. She embraced the whole experience." And was exactly the kind of woman he was looking for in a wife. Someone who shared his passion for this camp and those kids and was willing to work alongside him to make their dream come true.

"Sounds like you're just as smitten with her. No wonder she's planning to rejoin you for the Fourth."

"I'd be lying if I said I'm not looking forward to seeing her again."

"Well, she's got the whole week off, so you'll have plenty of time to show her around."

After another round of thank-yous from Daniel, they said their goodbyes.

Daniel immediately wanted to call Blythe, not only to thank her, but to share this incredible moment with her.

He glanced at the clock. It was 4:00 p.m. She'd still be at the office, so calling her might not be the best option. Instead, he sent her a text.

Call me when you're off work.

With excitement bubbling inside of him like a shaken-up can of soda, he sent up a prayer of thanksgiving then put his SUV in gear and headed for the ranch. At least he'd be able to share his good news with someone, even if it was just Noah.

A short time later, he bumped over the cattle guard

at Abundant Blessings Ranch feeling as though he was truly abundantly blessed. He wound past the stable and up the drive, dust billowing in his wake.

What was Hillary's SUV doing here? She and Dad had driven it to Santa Fe.

That could only mean one thing.

The old man exited the house as Daniel stepped from his vehicle.

"You just couldn't stay away, could you?" Daniel tossed his door closed.

"What can I say?" Pausing at the top step, his father shrugged. "We got bored."

"Bored? Seriously? Dad, I'm afraid that officially makes you a stick-in-the-mud."

"Yeah, well, I'd be happy for a little mud. Things are just getting way too dry around here."

Daniel understood his father's anxiety. After all, he'd lived with the cattle rancher his entire life. "Where's Hillary?"

"Inside freshening up." Dad poked a thumb toward the door.

"Well, if you don't mind, I have some news I'd like to share with the two of you."

They made their way inside, toeing out of their boots and shoes in the mudroom before moving into the family room.

Hillary emerged from the hallway. "Daniel." Smiling, she approached him for a hug.

"How was your trip?" He met her dark gaze.

"It was lovely. But it's good to be back home."

"The boy says he's got some news for us." Dad eased into his recliner.

"Does this news have anything to do with Blythe?"

Hillary moved to the sofa and motioned for Daniel to sit beside her.

"In a way." Because without her high praises, he might not have gotten even one year of additional funding. "She's going to be coming back out here for the Fourth."

"Oh, good." Hillary clasped her hands together. "She really is a darling. But then, I think you know that." She winked. "Is she going to stay here? Because if so, I'll need to get a room ready for her."

"Hmm... I guess I've been so focused on the camp I kind of forgot about finding her a place to stay."

"That's all right, dear. She's more than welcome to stay here. Or she could stay at my condo in town."

Condo? He'd forgotten all about that. "What are your plans for your condo? I mean, long-term. Are you going to rent it out? Sell it?"

"Actually, your father and I were just talking about that on our drive home. I know you've talked about moving out. I'm not sure what you had in mind, but if you're interested in the condo—"

"Yes."

The corners of her mouth lifted. "Well, all right then."

"If you two are finished," his father said, "I'd kinda like to hear about this news you got."

Daniel chuckled and proceeded to tell them about Jack's phone call.

The old man's eyes went wider than Daniel had ever seen. "Five years?"

"I know. I could hardly believe it myself."

"What an incredible blessing." Hillary pressed a hand to her chest. "They've basically removed that burden, allowing you to focus completely on the camp. Have you told Blythe yet?"

"I have not, though I'm sure she already knows. I told her to call me after she gets off work."

"This calls for a celebration," said Hillary. "Shall we grill or go out?"

"Grill," he and his father said collectively.

Hillary shook her head. "I should have known."

Daniel's phone rang, and he tugged it from his pocket to see Blythe's name on the screen. "I'll take this outside." He tapped the button and pressed the phone to his ear on his way into the mudroom. "Hello."

"Hello yourself." The smile in her voice made his grow even wider.

After pulling on his shoes he went outside. "I guess you know Jack called me." He continued off the deck and toward the barn.

"Oh, yeah. The guy could hardly wait. As soon as the board members were gone, he went straight to his office and closed the door."

"Blythe, I don't know what you said in that report, but thank you. To get one year of extra funding would have been great, but to not have to worry about anything but the camp for five years… That's beyond amazing."

"No," she said calmly, "that's God."

He couldn't help laughing. "You are correct, lovely lady. But I still owe you a debt of gratitude. So, when you get back out here, I'm going to be your personal tour guide and take you anywhere you want to go."

"Daniel, as long as I'm with you, anyplace will be an adventure."

Chapter Sixteen

"*A*re-are you sure?" *Blythe stared at the sonographer, imploring her to say no.*

"*Yes. You'll need to see an oncologist for a biopsy.*"

The whole scene seemed to run on a continuous loop through Blythe's mind, taunting her as she sat on her sister's gray microfiber couch the following afternoon, the sun spilling through arched windows as Blythe blinked away another round of tears. This couldn't be happening. Not now. She was in love and, for the first time in forever, actually contemplating a future. Marriage, kids, the whole shebang.

Now that future had come to a screeching halt. The fantasy gone in a cloud of dust.

Her mammogram this morning had revealed a suspicious growth and a subsequent ultrasound confirmed that Blythe would need to see an oncologist for a biopsy. From there, she could only imagine. A mastectomy, chemo… And just when she'd found a new outlook on life.

She should have stayed on the safe side of the street. *Like that would have stopped the cancer.*

Jenna dropped beside her with a fresh box of tissues, her own eyes rimmed red. Thankfully, her boys were gone, playing at their friends' houses. "I know this is scary, Blythe, but we can't keep dwelling on the worst-case scenario. I mean, they check you every year. This growth could turn out to be totally benign."

"But what if it's not?" Blythe grabbed another tissue. "I'd rather fear the worst and be pleasantly surprised than the other way around."

"So, the glass is half-empty." Her sister sent her one of those matter-of-fact looks.

"What?"

"You're being a pessimist," Jenna said emphatically.

Blythe glared long and hard at her sister, longing to rail against her. Jenna had no clue what it was like to have cancer. To be labeled as sick or fragile or different. She didn't know the stress and fatigue of treatments or the angst of wondering whether or not they would work.

This time, Blythe was looking at the possibility of a mastectomy, being injected with poisons, losing her hair… None of which presented a pretty picture. So, what did Jenna expect her to do? Say *ç'est la vie* and move on down the road?

She turned away, unable to look at her healthy, vibrant sister. The one who had everything going for her. A loving husband, two healthy kids… "Let's see how optimistic you are if you or one of your kids is ever diagnosed with cancer." Her words were unfair, she knew that. But cancer wasn't fair, either.

"That's just it, Blythe, you haven't been diagnosed yet." In true Jenna fashion, she ignored Blythe's rebuff, grabbed her shoulders instead and forced Blythe to look at her. "I don't want you to have cancer again. And I'm going to pray my little heart out that you won't. Why can't you cling to that same hope?"

"Because I've seen the reality of cancer. Not just my own, but in my peers."

Jenna let go then, her expression going flat. "You're talking about Miranda, aren't you?"

Blythe nodded, tears spilling anew as she thought about all her friend had endured those last months. Treatment, surgeries... "She was my best friend."

"I know, honey. But that was more than a decade ago. Scientists are discovering new treatments and cures every day."

She scowled at her sister. "Jenna, there is no cure for cancer."

"Not yet. But who's to say there won't be one today or tomorrow?"

Blythe pushed to her feet. Hugging herself, she paced across the colorful area rug and onto the wooden floor to stare out the window. Children raced their bikes around the cul-de-sac, laughing; a woman jogged along the sidewalk, pushing a stroller; a neighbor mowed his lawn. Happy, uninterrupted lives.

She took in a deep breath and turned away to see her sister still on the couch, wearing shorts and a T-shirt, knee drawn to her chest as she no doubt contemplated how to fix this.

Blythe had come to Jenna's because Jenna had always been there for her. She was the calm in Blythe's storm. The voice of reason. Until today, when that storm raged with such ferocity that Blythe was willing to ignore any and all reason.

Rubbing her arms, Blythe said, "I'm scared, Jenna."

The confession unleashed even more tears as her sister hurried to her side to comfort her.

"I know you are, sweetie." She enfolded Blythe in her embrace. "I am, too. But we can't let that fear rule us. Somehow, we have to find a way to release it to God and trust Him with the circumstances. No matter how horrible they might seem."

Blythe pulled back then. "You sound like Daniel. If he were here, he would tell me this is an opportunity to trust." Something she'd vowed to do only days ago when her life seemed so promising. Now her faith was crumbling faster than a house of cards.

"Speaking of Daniel, when are you going to tell him?"

"I'm not." She returned to the sofa. "Nor am I going to go back out there for the Fourth."

Her sister's brown eyes widened. "But you're looking forward to it."

"That was yesterday. This is today. I can't go back to Ouray and pretend this—" she motioned over her torso "—doesn't exist."

Moving to the edge of the couch, Jenna crossed her arms over her chest, jerking her head back. "You think cancer is going to change the way Daniel feels about you?"

"Of course, it will."

"It doesn't have to." Her sister lowered her arms. "You've already discussed the will-I-or-will-I-not-be-able-to-have-kids elephant in the room."

"Yes, but now I'm looking at the likelihood of losing a breast. Not to mention my hair, eyebrows and eyelashes." She ticked each one off on her fingers. "Daniel and I only met a few weeks ago. Do you really think he'll want to deal with all of that?"

"If he loves you, yes." Jenna's expression never shifted, not one iota as she eased beside Blythe. "After all you told me about Daniel the other night, I find it hard to believe he'd be so shallow as to reject you because of cancer."

"Uh, weren't you the one who thought he was just using me to get his camp funded?"

"That was *before* I heard all about your time with him." Jenna pulled her long dark ponytail over her shoulder and combed it with her fingers. A nervous habit Blythe readily recognized.

And, oddly, it comforted Blythe.

"Sweetie, this guy sounds like the kind of guy every woman dreams of finding. And given his heart for cancer patients, his history with his mother—she had breast cancer for crying out loud—I doubt your diagnosis is going to change his feelings for you."

"First, he watched his mother *die* from breast cancer. I will not put him through that again. Second, maybe I'm the one who's changed."

"Reverted is more like it." Jenna bolted to her feet. "You've gone back into protective mode. You're comfortable there because you think you can keep everyone at arm's length. And if you do that, you won't be hurt."

Blythe stared blankly at her sister. "Let's think about this, Jenna. Would you rather protect yourself or be hurt?"

"You're not being fair to Daniel. At least give the guy a chance. You've already envisioned a worst-case scenario *and* mentally cut him out of your life. At this point, what have you got to lose?"

* * *

By noon Thursday, Daniel found himself acting like a fool. Moping around, feeling all out of sorts. All because he hadn't heard from Blythe since yesterday morning. Even his numerous texts had yet to receive a response.

Yep, definitely foolish. The woman had work to do. She'd been away from the Ridley Foundation for almost three weeks, after all. Given that she was taking next week off, too, she probably had a serious amount of catching up to do.

But couldn't she at least respond to his texts?

Cool your jets. She'll be back in just a couple of days.

Yes, she would. And Daniel could hardly wait. He'd grown accustomed to seeing her smiling face every day, and he longed to make her a permanent part of his life. With her by his side, there was no telling what Camp Sneffels could become.

He went back to studying Adventure Haven. Since learning the camp would be funded for five years, he kept coming back up here, looking at things through a different lens. Improvements, new additions. Contemplating what would be most appealing to the kids. Not to mention appropriate for all ages, which was part of the reason he couldn't wait to talk to Blythe. He wanted to get her input.

The sun was high as cirrus clouds stretched across a crisp blue sky, but it wasn't overly warm. A perfect day to be in the mountains. Lord willing, the weather would be this nice next week. He had a whole list of things he wanted to do with Blythe. Places he wanted to show her. Adventures he itched to share with her.

Normally, white water rafting would be at the top of

his list, but given their dry weather, that was unlikely this year. The Uncompahgre was too low. He'd have to talk with some of his buddies to see how the San Miguel and Gunnison rivers were running. He didn't need uber adventure, just enough to give Blythe a taste of the experience.

His cell phone sounded in his pocket.

Hoping to see Blythe's name on the screen, he yanked the device from his shorts. Hmm… He didn't recognize the number but decided to answer it anyway.

"Hello."

"Is this Daniel?"

Curiosity had his gaze narrowing. "Yes. Can I help you?" He perused the challenge course. A new rope bridge would make a cool addition there.

"This is John Whitaker, Chloe's father."

Daniel's gut tightened. He'd been hoping for some news on Chloe but, so far, there'd been nothing.

"John, hey. How's Chloe doing?"

"I'm sorry I wasn't in touch sooner, but our lives have been kind of turned upside down since we left Camp Sneffels."

Daniel froze.

"Chloe has an aggressive sarcoma."

Daniel's eyes fell closed, his whole being suddenly heavy. Sarcoma. The word was scary enough alone. Throw in the word aggressive…

Lowering himself to the ground, he shoved a hand through his hair. "I—I'm sorry to hear that, John." This was not the outcome he'd wanted. The outcome he'd prayed for.

"So were we. However, there is some good news."

"Oh?" Daniel rested his elbows atop his bent knees.

"There's an experimental treatment the doctors are quite hopeful about."

"That sounds encouraging."

"Very. And now that she's stable, Chloe, Amanda and I will be heading to Aurora for her first round."

"Aurora? That's not far from Denver. Perhaps Blythe could stop by and visit."

"Chloe would love that. She's still talking about Blythe and Evie. Not to mention zip-lining."

Daniel couldn't help thinking about Blythe. "Seems zip-lining was a high point for a lot of lives this summer."

"You've got a great camp there, Daniel. Don't stop doing what you're doing, because you're making a difference in these kids' lives."

"I appreciate that, John. And thank you for sharing Chloe with us. Meeting her was truly a blessing." When their call ended, Daniel lay back on the bed of pine needles and stared into the trees.

God, please be with Chloe. And, if it's in Your will, I pray that she would be healed from this dreaded disease.

He'd need to inform Blythe of the situation. No doubt, she'd want to see Chloe.

His phone rang again.

Sitting up, he noticed Jack Hendershot's name on the screen.

He drew in what he hoped was a cleansing breath before answering. "Hey, Jack, what's up?"

"Have you talked to Blythe lately?"

Daniel pushed to his feet. "No, not since yesterday morning." His heart began to thud. "Why? Is there a problem?" Something that kept her from answering his texts. Maybe she was hurt or—

"I don't know what to think, but something's just not right, Daniel."

Fear rose inside of him. "Not right how? What happened?"

"For two days Blythe seemed like a changed woman. Then she came in this morning, hair pulled back tight again, as though trying to show the world she was in control. But something had her rattled. She asked to take the rest of the day off. Said there was something she had to do. And this was *after* she took off yesterday afternoon."

Blythe was off, yet she hadn't communicated with Daniel at all.

"That's not like her, Daniel. I know she had a doctor's appointment yesterday morning, but she said it was just routine. Yet when she came in today, there was fear in her eyes." Jack hesitated. "Between you and me, it looked like she'd been crying."

Interesting. She hadn't said anything to Daniel about an appointment. Then again, if it had indeed been routine, why bother? Still, that didn't jive with her lack of communication with Daniel and the seemingly strange behavior Jack had observed.

"I don't know what to say, Jack. But if I hear something, I'll let you know. And if you don't mind, I'd appreciate the same courtesy from you. I care deeply about Blythe."

"That's part of the reason I called. Blythe came back from Ouray changed. And I believe you had a lot to do with that."

When the line went dead, Daniel promptly texted Blythe.

Miss you. How's it going?

To his surprise, she responded only seconds later.

Busy. Sorry, but I won't be able to make it back for the 4th.

Busy? With what? She wasn't at work.

His heart twisted. Something had changed her mind. Or maybe Jack was correct.

Something wasn't right. And Daniel had to do whatever he could to find out exactly what was going on.

Chapter Seventeen

Blythe retrieved the Camp Sneffels folder from her desk Friday morning and tucked it into the file drawer of her credenza. If only she could rid her mind of the memories that easily. Good memories. Happy ones that now served only to taunt her, reminding her of what might have been.

She eased into her desk chair, ready to start on her next project. Perhaps that would distract her from all of the depressing thoughts floating through her head.

Opening the file on her computer, she hated that she'd bowed out of work both Wednesday afternoon and yesterday. That was not like her at all. But she hadn't known what else to do. She'd been a mess after her appointment and yesterday she'd been forced to find a new oncologist thanks to the retirement of her former doctor. And even though she'd finally found one who would take her insurance, they couldn't get her in for three weeks. Three very long, excruciating weeks. Meaning she'd just have to keep herself busy so she wouldn't have time to dwell.

She stared at the computer screen. At least inner-city literacy programs wouldn't be so draining.

"Blythe?"

Her fingers hovered over the keyboard as unwanted tears pricked the backs of her eyes. That voice did not belong here. It belonged in Ouray, at Camp Sneffels. Why would Daniel be here?

Turning, she glimpsed the handsome adventurer standing in her doorway. Strange, for as much as she'd thought about him since returning to Denver, her mind had failed to recall just how good-looking he truly was.

"What are you doing here?" She remained seated for fear she'd be tempted to throw herself into his strong arms.

He moved to the opposite side of her desk. "I need to talk to you. Is there someplace we can go? Outside, perhaps?"

"I'm sorry, but I have work—"

"Daniel?" Jack stepped into her office. "I thought that was you." He extended a hand.

Daniel promptly shook it. "Hey, Jack. Good to see you again."

"What brings you to Denver?" Jack smiled, his eyes shifting to Blythe. "Or should I say who?"

She wanted to disappear under her desk. But given it was made of glass, that wouldn't do her much good.

Hands slung low on his gray-denim-clad hips, Daniel said, "I need to discuss something with Blythe." He glanced her way before continuing. "Would you mind if we stepped out of the building for a little bit?"

How dare he go over her head. "I just said—"

"Of course not." Her boss moved aside as though he'd been blocking their exit. "Take all the time you need.

There's not much going on around here today, what with the long holiday weekend coming up."

"I wouldn't ask if it wasn't important," Daniel added.

"Not a problem." Jack started out the door. "You kids have fun."

Fun? Was he joking?

She stared at Daniel. Rarely had she seen his expression so serious. Almost pained. Was it because she'd all but cut off communication with him?

"This really is important, Blythe," he finally said.

With a deep breath, she pushed her chair back and stood, grabbing her purse on the way out the door. They made their way down to the lobby and out to the little courtyard between the building and the parking garage in silence. Not even any small talk.

She sat on one of the wooden benches. "Daniel, I'm sorry I've been so distant—"

"That's not what I wanted to talk to you about." He took a seat beside her. "Though don't think it hasn't been on my mind."

In that moment, her heart ached for him. She should have just told him they were done. But she hadn't had the strength.

Elbows on his thighs, he glanced her way before studying the rose bush opposite them. "I received a call from Chloe's father yesterday."

Blythe's heart raced, her hands growing clammy as fear swept over her. Daniel would not come all this way with good news.

Closing her eyes, she clasped her hands in her lap and did her best to steel herself.

"Chloe has been diagnosed with an aggressive sarcoma." He continued, mentioning something about treatment, but his words faded into nothingness.

Everything except *sarcoma*. That one little word had robbed her of what little strength she might have possessed. Chloe had a sarcoma. Just like Miranda.

She pressed her lips tightly together to keep from sobbing as hot tears streaked down her cheeks. Her body shook with the effort to keep everything inside.

But when Daniel's warm hand covered her frozen fingers, everything let loose and her grief flooded out.

"Why?" she wailed. "Why?"

He wrapped his arms around her and tried to console her, but there was too much sorrow to be contained. For Chloe, for Miranda and for herself. Cancer was evil. A vicious attacker claiming one innocent life after another. Tearing apart families and laying waste to hopes and dreams. She hated the dreaded disease with every fiber of her being.

"Come on," Daniel said as he lifted her to her feet. "Let's get you out of here."

Twenty minutes ago, she would have argued with him; now she didn't have the strength. He loaded her into his SUV, then climbed behind the wheel.

"Give me your address."

When his words finally registered, she tearfully complied before another round of anguish enveloped her. The next thing she knew, they were pulling up to her apartment building.

"How?" Then she recalled hearing a voice coming from his phone. He'd typed her address into the GPS.

She struggled to open her door until Daniel intervened.

He helped her out of the vehicle, but still held her close. "Which way are we headed?"

She pointed to the building in front of them. "Second floor." Her chin trembled, making her words come out shaky. "Number tw-twenty-two twenty-five."

Once they were inside, Blythe grabbed the furry pink blanket from the back of her sofa and wrapped it around her. She was so cold.

"Can I get you anything?" Daniel never left her side.

"No, I'm—" The sight of the Camp Sneffels T-shirt draped over the back of one of her dining chairs had her pain swelling once more. At least this time her tears were silent. "First Miranda, now Chloe. What is wrong with me?"

"Miranda?" Daniel looked confused. "She was your friend from your camp, right?"

She nodded. "Our friendship continued even after camp. And we were *so* close." She sniffed. "Then Miranda was diagnosed with a sarcoma and—" Her voice cracked. "She was gone."

"Oh, Blythe." He pulled her close and held her. When her cries rose again, he scooped her up, carried her to the couch and remained at her side. "I know you miss your friend, but this is good news with Chloe. Not only is she still with us, but the treatments—"

She shot to her feet. "They said the same thing about Miranda."

"That was years ago." He stared up at her. "Things have come a long way since then. I don't understand why you can't be more hopeful."

"Because life doesn't always turn out the way we want it to."

"I'm aware of that. But I still believe God has a plan.

At least Chloe is willing to fight. You've given up on her. As someone once said to me, where's your faith?"

Anger swelled within her. "What happened to Miranda wasn't right. What Chloe's going through isn't right. So, forgive me, but how am I supposed to trust God when He allows stuff like that to happen?"

Without so much as flinching, Daniel said, "Jesus was without sin. Yet He was nailed to a cross and died so that sinners like us could live."

They stared at each other for the longest time. Until Daniel finally said, "Why did you decide not to come back to Ouray?"

Forcing herself not to look away, she said, "I have breast cancer."

Daniel felt as though he'd been punched in the gut. Air whooshed from his lungs, and he wanted to double over from the agony of Blythe's words.

Breast cancer. The very thing that had stolen his mother away. But not before she'd pushed through the torture of two surgeries and multiple rounds of chemotherapy. Watching Mama slowly fade away was the most excruciating experience of Daniel's life. One he never wanted to go through again.

Until now.

If Blythe had cancer he wanted to fight this battle with her, alongside her, carrying her, if need be. But, oh, how he prayed they would be victorious.

Standing, he moved around the glass-topped coffee table until he was beside her. "When did you find this out?"

"Wednesday." Clearing her throat, she tossed the blanket aside and squared her shoulders, woefully attempting to be brave. "It was supposed to be a routine mammogram. But there was nothing routine about it. Now I'm just waiting to see an oncologist, but a mastectomy will likely be in order. Probably chemotherapy—"

"Whoa, hold on." He held up a hand. "You haven't even seen your cancer doctor, and you're already assuming the worst?"

Though her eyes were still rimmed with red, her tears had vanished. Her expression was very matter-of-fact. "I'm just trying to keep things real."

"Well, you're not doing a very good job of it." He studied her a moment: the tailored navy pantsuit with the white button-down blouse, the slicked-back hair, although it was now slightly disheveled. This was not the Blythe he'd come to know and love. This was the Blythe who sought to control every aspect of her life. The one who played things safe. The one who refused to take any risks. And love was a big risk. Especially with her life suddenly spiraling out of control.

His eyes never left her. "Why didn't you tell me, Blythe? I mean, we're supposed to be in a relationship here. Or at least that's what I thought. People who care about each other share things, good or bad, so they can weather the storms together."

"Perhaps." She picked up the blanket and began to fold it. "Or maybe it's just better to end things and go our separate ways."

He couldn't believe his ears. "Do you really believe that? Better for who, anyway? Certainly not me. I don't want to be separated from you, Blythe. These last few days without you have been unbearable. And proved to me the one thing I suspected all along."

She set the blanket over the arm of the white chair. "What's that?"

"That not only do I love you, I want to share my life with you." He heard her quick intake of air, but she quickly recovered.

Moving to the window to the right of the small fireplace, she said, "That's when you thought I was healthy."

"Oh, like that's supposed to make a difference." Incredulous, he made his way across the beige carpet until he was behind her. "I told you I loved you, Blythe, and I meant it. Do you think cancer is going to change how I feel about you? Like love is something I can just switch on and off at will?"

She continued to peer through the blinds, refusing to look at him.

Reaching out, he rubbed her upper arms. "Don't do this, Blythe. Don't shut me out. Please."

"I'm not shutting you out, Daniel. I'm *giving* you an out."

He turned her to face him then, the fruity, floral scent of her perfume enveloping him as he encouraged her to meet his gaze. "I don't want out. I want to be right here beside you. Forever."

Her hazel eyes searched his and, for a moment, he dared to hope. "I'm sorry, Daniel. That's something I just can't do. Because forever doesn't come with a guarantee."

He let go a sigh and touched his forehead to hers. "I know you're afraid, Blythe. Cancer is scary. But would you rather be afraid alone or together with someone who's willing to walk through the fire with you?"

She pulled away then, pain marring her beautiful

features. Turning on her high-heeled shoes, she moved from the living room, past the open kitchen and dining area to the spot where they'd entered. She twisted the deadbolt and swung open the door.

"I think it would be best if you leave."

His heart ached in so many different ways. Standing in her nicely appointed living room where nothing was out of place, he couldn't help feeling as though he'd let her down. Blythe was hurting. Big-time. And there was nothing he could do to stop it or make it better. Nothing she'd allow him to do. Leaving him with only one option.

He moved to the door. "Would you like me to take you back to work?"

"No, I'm good."

He surreptitiously shook his head. Blythe was anything but good. Her world was crashing in. Because of Chloe, because of Miranda… Because of the uncertainty hovering over her like a storm cloud. And it was tearing him apart to watch her withdraw. He didn't want to go. He wanted to be with her, comfort her, care for her.

But that wasn't what Blythe wanted. So he would go and pray that somehow, someway, she would come to her senses and reach out to him.

Looking down at her, seeing the unspoken terror in her eyes, a lump formed in his throat. He struggled to swallow it away.

"Just so you'll know, Dr. Joel is one of the top cancer doctors in the nation. And he's just up the road from Ouray, in Montrose. I'm sure he'd be more than happy to see you." With that, he pressed a kiss to her forehead. "Goodbye, Blythe."

It took every ounce of willpower Daniel possessed to turn and propel himself down the stairs. He despised that he was walking away. Even though it didn't mean he was giving up.

Blythe—the real Blythe with the tender heart and newfound passion for life—was too precious to give up on. He'd give her time to work through the grieving process and then he'd be back.

What if she pushes you away again?

Then he might have to start pushing back.

Crossing the parking lot, he clicked the fob to unlock his SUV.

He would not let Blythe go without a fight. She needed him as much as he and Camp Sneffels needed her. Maybe even more. So, for now, he would help her fight this battle on his knees, praying God would not only heal her, but bring her back. And when that happened, Daniel would never let her go again.

Chapter Eighteen

B lythe moved into her bedroom and watched out the window as Daniel got into his SUV. He was gone. On his way back to Ouray. Without her.

Isn't that what you wanted?

Yes. No. She dropped her head into her hands. *I don't know what I want.*

The tears that had nearly choked her as she struggled to keep them hidden while saying goodbye to Daniel now streamed down her face. She'd cried so much these last few days that she was surprised she had any tears left. And yet they seemed to keep coming.

She thought about Chloe and her brilliant smile as she zoomed through the trees on the zip line. The way she'd been willing to put aside her own desires for her friend. And how she had touched Blythe's heart.

Tugging off her jacket, she dropped onto the side of the bed. Why did Chloe have to get sick? The question played on a continuous loop through her mind until she thought she might go mad. She needed to go back to work. Whether she wanted to or not. She'd missed too much time already. And maybe it would help to focus her mind on something else.

Hearing her phone ring, she hurried into the other room and scrambled to retrieve it from her purse before it went to voice mail.

"Hello?"

"Why aren't you at work?" Jenna scolded on the other end of the line.

"How do you know that?"

"Because I just dropped by with lunch and you weren't there."

She kicked out of her shoes. "I'm at home."

"And I can tell you've been crying. I'm on my way."

Twenty minutes later, she and Jenna were standing beside her wood and metal bistro table, unpacking the chicken nuggets and waffle fries Jenna had brought.

"So, adventure boy showed up at your office?" Jenna and her nicknames.

"Yes. Remember the little girl I told you about? Chloe? The one that got sick and had to leave camp."

"Uh-huh." Jenna bit into a waffle fry.

Blythe lifted a shoulder, trying to maintain her composure. Or at least what little was left of it. "She has a sarcoma."

Her sister's dark eyes widened. "Oh, no." She promptly dusted off her hands and stretched her arms around Blythe. "Are they going to be able to treat it?"

"They're going to try." Blythe pulled away. "She was such a precious girl." She'd taught Blythe to feel again. Although, right now, all she wanted was to feel nothing.

Reaching for a nugget, Jenna shot her a curious glance. "What do you mean *was*? Chloe is *still* a precious girl."

Peeling off the top of a special sauce cup, Blythe froze as Daniel's words played across her mind. *You've given up on her.* She remembered staying by Chloe's side while she was sick at camp, holding her hand, doing whatever she could to make her comfortable and praying that she would be all right. Now she'd all but written Chloe off.

"Yes, that's what I meant."

Jenna pulled out an industrial-style chair and sat down. "What I don't get is why Daniel came all the way to Denver to tell you."

Blythe grabbed her lidded cup of lemonade and took her own seat. "Because I hadn't answered any of his calls or responded to his texts, except to tell him that I wouldn't be back out there for the Fourth."

One of Jenna's dark brows lifted. "And…did he bring that up?"

Nodding, Blythe grabbed a nugget and filled her sister in on the details of their conversation.

"Good grief, Blythe." Jenna fell back in her chair. "Do you have any idea how many women would love to have a man like that? Someone you can count on to be there through thick and thin. Someone with the heart of a hero."

Blythe dunked a nugget in the sauce before popping it into her mouth. "I know."

"Uh, no. Obviously you don't. Otherwise you wouldn't have sent him away. Especially when you're in love with him, too. For crying out loud, what is wrong with you?"

Blythe rolled her puffy eyes. "We've been over this. I don't want to burden him."

"Stop acting as though you're doing Daniel some big favor by letting him go. You're being selfish, Blythe.

Yes, love involves risk. But shouldn't *he* be the one to decide if he's willing to hang around or not?"

Blythe found herself blinking rapidly again. "I don't want to end up hurt."

Her sister heaved an exasperated sigh. "Baby girl, you are your own worst enemy." Reaching across the table, she took hold of Blythe's hand. "You're already hurting. For once, can't you allow yourself to be happy?"

"I was, while I was at camp. I don't think I've ever been happier. And I can't tell you how free I felt. Like I could do almost anything."

The brow arched higher this time. "I don't suppose Daniel had anything to do with that, did he?"

As much as she wanted to deny it… "He encouraged me. Supported me. Believed in me." She grabbed a waffle fry and dunked it in some ketchup. "Outside of you, he's the only person who's ever done that."

"And you loved him for it."

Blythe stared absently at the uneaten fry. "No. I love him for it." She lifted her gaze to her sister's. "I still love him, Jenna."

Her sister smiled. "I was wondering when you were going to figure that out. Question is, what are you going to do about it?"

"I'm not sure." Blythe gathered up her trash and took it into the kitchen.

Dr. Joel is one of the top cancer doctors in the nation.

She liked Dr. Joel. And since she was being forced to find a new doctor anyway…

Except that would mean returning to Ouray. And at the moment, that was a terrifying thought. She'd sent Daniel on his way. Wouldn't it be best to leave well enough alone?

"You could start by having a little more faith in the guy," her sister offered.

"Since when have I ever been good at exercising any kind of trust?"

What about when you were on that zip line?

Blythe stopped short of the wastebasket.

She had trusted, hadn't she? In a piece of equipment, no less.

Stepping on the foot pedal to lift the lid, she dropped the trash in the receptacle and swallowed hard. *God, You know trust doesn't come easy to me. Help me. Teach me how to trust in You and in Daniel.*

She turned and started for the bathroom to fix her hair and her face. "Jenna, I need you to take me back to work. But first, I need to make a phone call."

Daniel sat in the camp office Saturday afternoon, a warm breeze sifting through the open windows as he stared at a twelve-month calendar without really seeing it at all. He'd come up there mostly so he could be alone. But he also wanted to nail down dates for next year's camps. Yet no matter how hard he tried to focus, his mind kept wandering back to Denver and a certain hazel-eyed woman who'd laid claim to his heart.

Yesterday Blythe had complained that Chloe's sarcoma wasn't right. Well, it wasn't right that Blythe was facing cancer for a second time, either. And it wasn't right that she was punishing Daniel when all he wanted to do was help.

I'm giving you an out.

No, she wasn't. She was pushing him away. Was she that eager to be rid of him?

In his heart he knew better. She was afraid that he would change his mind. Didn't she know him better than that?

Closing his eyes, he bowed his head. *Lord, forgive me for complaining. I vowed to pray for Blythe and that's what I will do. Besides, complaining will get me nowhere, while prayer can move mountains. And in Blythe's eyes, that lump is as big as a mountain.*

Be with her. Comfort her as only You can. Lord, I pray that the spot they found is not cancer. That her fears would be for nothing and that, somehow, You would bring us back together. I do love her, and I thank You for bringing her into my life. Amen.

Looking up, he noticed a grosbeak sitting just outside the window beside his desk. The black-and-yellow bird peered straight at him, cocking its head left then right before breaking into a sweet song that washed over Daniel, imparting a peace that hadn't been there before.

Maybe now he'd be able to focus.

Looking at the calendar, he knew he wanted to have at least four camps the next year, though they might be able to pull off five or six. As always, volunteers would be key. Could he find enough companions to cover that many weeks? He'd had more than enough this year, but that had only been for two weeks.

The sound of gravel being ground beneath tires drifted through the open window behind his desk. He wasn't expecting anyone, so if he had to guess, he'd say it was either Levi, Dad or one of his brothers. Or simply someone who was lost. The latter had him reminding himself to shut the gate now that the camp was closed.

Standing, he rounded his desk, moved to the front door and continued onto the porch as a white Camry appeared at the far end of the office.

Blythe?

His heart thundered against his ribs. Why was she here? Had she changed her mind? Did she want to be with him after all?

Don't get your hopes up.

But—she's here! That alone was a good sign, wasn't it?

He watched as she parked in the shade of a blue spruce and got out of her vehicle, all the while trying to remain calm. Inside, though, he wanted to run to her, scoop her into his arms and kiss her senseless. Instead, he simply smiled as she moved toward him.

Dressed in a pair of white shorts, a sleeveless black-and-white checked shirt and sandals, she wore her hair down. And there was something different in her countenance. Her pinched expression of yesterday had been replaced with a sense of calm. She looked...at peace.

He leaned against one of the posts as she neared the porch. "What brings you up here?"

The corners of her mouth tilted ever so slightly upward. "Well, somebody told me about this really cool Fourth of July celebration they have in Ouray." She climbed the steps and stopped in front of him.

Peering down at her, he thought his chest might explode. "You said you weren't coming."

She lifted a shoulder. "I know, but since I have an appointment with Dr. Joel on the fifth, I figured...why not?"

Dr. Joel? That would mean—

"Besides, there's something I need to tell you." Her eyes sparkled up at him.

"What's that?"

"I love you, too."

With his heart racing, he lowered his head and touched his lips to hers before wrapping his arms around her and crushing her against him. When he finally came up for air, they both had tears in their eyes.

"How did the doctor get you in so quick?"

"It was the strangest thing." Her arms were still looped around his neck. "When I called them yesterday afternoon, they said they'd just had a cancellation."

"Sounds like divine intervention to me." He tugged her closer.

"God has a plan for me, Daniel. I've rebelled against that fact for far too long and tried to make my own way. Instead, I only made myself miserable. Until I met you. Falling in love with you wasn't part of my design, but it was part of God's. And whether I'm on this earth for one more year or a hundred, I'd really like to have you in my life."

He threaded his fingers into her soft hair, cupping her cheek. "However many days He gives us. I would rather have you in my life for a little while than never have you at all." He swallowed the lump that threatened his composure. "Will you marry me, Blythe, and allow me the honor of being at your side through every step of this journey?"

A tear spilled onto her cheek, and he wiped it away with his thumb. "Chemo will ensure I won't be able to have any children."

"We'll cross that bridge if and when we come to it. Besides, this isn't about children, Blythe. It's about you and me. So, what do you say?"

Her lips quivered as the corners of her beautiful mouth lifted. "Okay."

He pulled her to him and savored the beautiful woman God had ordained expressly for him. He didn't know what their future held, but he knew beyond a shadow of a doubt Who held their future. And that was something he could count on forever.

Epilogue

U nder a golden late-afternoon sun, Blythe stood amid
the wildflowers in the meadow surrounding the lake
at Camp Sneffels. She'd never been happier or more at
peace. Even her looming biopsy results couldn't stop
her from smiling. In part because she'd determined to
entrust her circumstances to God. Something that was a
daily, if not moment-by-moment choice. Still, she knew
He held each and every one of her days in His mighty
hand.

Of course, the fact that she was wearing a sleeveless white-lace gown and was in the process of marrying the man of her dreams had a good bit to do with
her smile, too.

Holding hands with her handsome groom, a diamond
band sparkling on her left hand, she anxiously awaited
the words she'd been longing to hear for the past three
weeks.

"By the power vested in me by God and the State
of Colorado, I now pronounce you husband and wife."
Pastor Dan smiled at Daniel. "You may kiss your bride."

A grinning Daniel wasted no time. He promptly

tugged her against him and claimed her lips while family and friends cheered them on.

"I am crazy in love with you, Blythe," he said when they parted.

"Right back atcha, my love."

Moments later, the pastor turned them to face their guests. "It is my distinct pleasure to introduce to you Mr. and Mrs. Daniel Stephens."

Applause filled the mountain air. On the front row of white folding chairs, Blythe's parents smiled proudly. Her mother dabbed a tissue to her eyes. When Blythe had told them about the new threat of cancer, they'd dropped everything and come to Colorado. To Ouray first, then to Denver to help Blythe move. She hadn't seen her folks since Christmas, and they seemed…different. Happier. According to her mother, they'd been going to marriage counseling, though Blythe had yet to find out why.

Whatever the case, Mom had accepted Daniel and his family without reservation or judgment. And she'd even apologized to Jenna and her husband, vowing to make up for lost time. Her mother's drastic turnaround had them feeling more like a family again. And that only added to Blythe's joy.

While pictures were taken, some guests remained while others caravanned back to the chow hall where dinner and dancing would continue into the evening. Juanita had insisted on doing the catering, saying if Daniel's mother had been here, it was what she would have wanted.

As the photo session wrapped up, Jack, her now former boss, approached with his wife.

"First, I just want to thank you two for providing an

excuse for me to get away and come see the camp first-hand. What you've done here is pretty amazing, Daniel."

"Thank you, Jack." He wrapped an arm around Blythe. "And I believe what God has done here is pretty amazing, too."

"Hear, hear! Although—" The man wagged a finger, his brows narrowing "—I am a little disappointed that I'm going to have to find another overseer."

"Well, Jack," said Blythe, "why don't you just appoint yourself? Not only would it get you out of the office more, it would give you an excuse to come and visit us."

"Oh, I like that idea," his wife was quick to add.

As sunlight faded, everyone made their way to the chow hall. The camp golf cart had been decorated with streamers, balloons and empty soda cans that rattled behind them as Daniel drove Blythe back.

While guests and family entered the building, Blythe and Daniel paused at the little cabin near the office. It had been adorned with flowers, lanterns, two chairs and even a faux firepit like they'd had at the school after the evacuation. When Daniel's sisters-in-law—make that *her* sisters-in-law—learned that was where they'd decided to spend their honeymoon, they'd banded together to turn the place into a romantic getaway.

Of course, if it was too inviting, they might never want to leave. And given that they'd already moved her things into Hillary's old condo—now the home she and Daniel would soon share—that might not be so good.

"I have something for you." Daniel reached into his jacket pocket and pulled out an envelope.

"What is it?" She watched him curiously.

"Open it and find out."

She lifted the flap of the white envelope with her

name on it and pulled out a glittery pink card that read Happy Wedding Day.

Smiling up at Daniel, she opened it before lowering her gaze.

Dear Blythe.
I'm SO happy that you and Daniel are getting married. Did he get down on one knee when he proposed? You know, like they do in the movies.

Blythe puffed out a laugh.

Thank you for taking care of me while I was at camp. I still have cancer, but I'm feeling better. Except for when I have treatments. Sometimes those aren't so fun. But my mom and dad say they're helping. I sure hope so, because I really want to come to Camp Sneffels again.
Love, Chloe

"Oh, Daniel." Dabbing her eyes, she peered up at him. "Chloe wants to come back to camp someday. I pray that she'll be able to."

"So do I. And this time, for the entire week."

"Amen to that."

He grinned down at her. "Well, Mrs. Stephens…" He cupped her cheek with his hand, threading his fingers into her hair. "Do you suppose we ought to make an appearance at our reception—" he nodded toward the chow hall "—or just hide out here?"

"Mm." She leaned into his caress as the sounds of nature whispered around them. "As much as I would *love* to stay here, I think they might find us."

"Ah. Good point." He kissed her lips with a tenderness that sent goosebumps shivering up her spine. "I love you, Blythe."

Staring into his blue eyes, she had no doubt that what he said was true. He was her hero. The man who saved her when she didn't even realize she needed saving. And with God as their guide, they would face whatever adventures lay ahead.

Daniel stared fondly at the camp directors' cabin, recalling the honeymoon he and Blythe had spent there a little over ten months ago. What was supposed to be a few days had turned into a week they'd never forget.

He still found it interesting that most of that time had been spent talking not so much about *their* future, but the future of Camp Sneffels. Blythe had so many ideas, even thoughts on how the camp could be utilized in the off-season for retreats, weddings and other special events. Her input was priceless, and Daniel wasn't sure what he'd do without her.

The cabin door opened then, and his lovely wife and codirector stepped onto the stoop, dressed more for a party than camp in her skinny jeans, flowing tunic and sparkly sandals. But then, that was exactly what today was—a party. An open house for the people of Ouray to come and see Camp Sneffels firsthand. After all the community had done to assist them when the camp had been evacuated the previous year, this was his and Blythe's way of saying thank-you with food, tours and plenty of fun.

Slipping an arm around her waist, he tugged her close. "You feeling okay?"

Her face practically glowed as she smiled up at him. "Never better." Blythe's fears of a mastectomy and chemotherapy had never come to pass because her biopsy had come back negative. She was still cancer free. And her—make that *their*—greatest dream was now coming true. They were expecting their first child in December. "However, these jeans are starting to get a bit snug."

"Sounds like we'd better do some shopping before camp starts, then."

The sound of gravel crunching under tires echoed through the air as the entire Stephens family rolled up the drive in their respective vehicles.

Daniel glanced at his watch. "Looks like they're right on time." Though his family thought they were to come early for some instruction, that was only part of the reason he wanted them there before everyone else.

Slowly, each of his brothers and their families exited their vehicles. Noah with Lily, twelve-year-old Colton, nine-year-old Piper and eight-month-old Joy; Andrew, Carly, fourteen-year-old Megan and twenty-one-month-old Lucas; Matt, Lacie, seven-year-old Kenzie and one-year-old Riley; and Jude with his wife, Kayla, and sixteen-month-old Avery.

"Why don't you all join me at the flagpole." He motioned for them to follow him and Blythe.

Standing in the family circle, Hillary grinned. "I don't know if you fellas have noticed, but this next generation of Stephens is predominantly girls."

"We've definitely gone through some changes," said Noah, holding baby Joy.

"We sure have." Dad tilted his beige cowboy hat back. "Five years ago, we didn't know how we'd make it." Holding his wife's hand, his dark gaze roamed the circle. "Look at us now."

Daniel took hold of Blythe's hand. "You're a blessed man, Dad."

"I surely am. God's been good to this old cowboy. And he's been good to you boys, too. Your mama would be proud."

Just the segue Daniel needed. "Speaking of Mama, the real reason I wanted all of you to come early was so Blythe and I could show you something." Still holding his wife's hand, he moved toward the new metal structure situated between the office and the chow hall. And while it was indeed metal, with the dark brown ridges positioned horizontally on the walls and a dark green roof, it looked like a log cabin.

He stopped beside the cloth-covered sign positioned in front of the cabin. "As I'm sure we all remember, Mama loved to craft. And she especially enjoyed scrapbooking." His gaze drifted to Andrew's wife. "Right, Carly?"

"Oh, yes. She was very meticulous about it." It was Carly who had discovered boxes of photos that had been set aside for Daniel and each of his brothers. Inside, Mama had laid everything out, including handwritten notes to her sons. Unfortunately, she'd passed before she was able to compile the scrapbooks, so Carly had finished them for her.

"So, when Blythe brought up the subject of a crafting spot for the campers—" something that had surprised him, given her camp experience, but she'd explained how it would provide an opportunity for the kids to take a break from all of their adventures and, perhaps, commemorate them "—and scrapbooking in particular, I knew what we had to do." He released his wife's hand. "I'll let you do the honors."

She moved to the sign, took hold of the cloth and waited for Daniel to continue.

"It is our hope that Mama's love for creating will live on with Camp Sneffels's newest addition." He gestured toward the cabin as Blythe unveiled the carved wooden sign. "Mona's Crafting Cottage."

The women gasped, then said, "Aww…" collectively, while his father and brothers stood silently, seemingly too moved to say anything.

Stepping onto the wooden porch, Daniel threw open the door. "Come check it out."

The women and kids rushed in, but the men lingered.

"I'll play tour guide." Blythe patted his arm and then went inside.

Clearing his throat, he rejoined his father and brothers. "What do you think?"

"I don't know about the rest of you guys," said Jude, "but I'm thinking about how I'm going to get back at you for getting me all choked up."

"No kidding." Matt swiped a hand under each eye.

Daniel turned to the patriarch of the Stephens clan who stood staring at the sign. "Dad?"

"I think it's a fitting tribute to a woman who blessed us with her faith and her passion for life. Your mother was a special woman. And her legacy lives on in each of us."

Daniel couldn't agree more. It was a legacy that had been passed down from generation to generation. Now it was time for him and his brothers to carry on that tradition with their children. Because with God, nothing was impossible.

* * * * *

Dear Reader,

Has your faith ever been tested? Have you ever been filled with fear in the face of scary circumstances? It's one thing to trust God when life is easy, but when we're facing the unknown, trust becomes a challenge. Especially if you tend to be a fixer, like me. Yet there are many things in this world that can't be fixed or controlled. It's then we either reject God or cling to The One who holds us and our future in His hands. Day by day, moment by moment.

Telling Blythe and Daniel's story was as difficult as it was fulfilling. Cancer is a word that can impart fear into the strongest person. Like the thief who comes to steal, kill and destroy, cancer has impacted many lives. Young, old, male, female… And I would love nothing more than to see this dreaded disease wiped off the face of this earth.

This was the final book in my Rocky Mountain Heroes series. I hope you enjoyed watching the Stephens men find love as much as I did. But there are plenty more relationships to explore, so I hope we'll meet again soon. Until then, I would love to hear from you. You can contact me via my website, mindyobenhaus.com, or you can snail-mail me c/o Love Inspired Books, 195 Broadway, 24th Floor, New York, NY 10007.

See you next time…
Mindy.

SPECIAL EXCERPT FROM

🌿

LOVE INSPIRED
INSPIRATIONAL ROMANCE

*Can the new teacher in this Amish community help the
family next door without losing her heart?*

Read on for a sneak preview of
The Amish Teacher's Dilemma *by Patricia Davids,
available in March 2020 from Love Inspired.*

Clang, clang, clang.

The hammering outside her new schoolhouse grew
louder. Eva Coblentz moved to the window to locate
the source of the clatter. Across the road she saw a man
pounding on an ancient-looking piece of machinery with
steel wheels and a scoop-like nose on the front end.

When he had the sheet of metal shaped to fit the front
of the machine, he stood back to assess his work. He
knelt and hammered on the shovel-like nose three more
times. Satisfied, he gathered up his tools and started in
her direction.

She stepped back from the window. Was he coming to
the school? Why? Had he noticed her gawking? Perhaps
he only wanted to welcome the new teacher, although his
lack of a beard said he wasn't married.

She glanced around the room. Should she meet him
by the door? That seemed too eager. Her eyes settled on
the large desk at the front of the classroom. She should
look as if she was ready for the school year to start. A
professional attitude would put off any suggestion that
she was interested in meeting single men.

LIEXP0220

Eva hurried to the desk, pulled out the chair and sat down as the outside door opened. The chair tipped over backward, sending her flailing. Her head hit the wall with a painful thud as she slid to the floor. Stunned, she slowly opened her eyes to see the man leaning over the desk.

He had the most beautiful gray eyes she'd ever beheld. They were rimmed with thick, dark lashes in stark contrast to the mop of curly, dark red hair springing out from beneath his straw hat. Tiny sparks of light whirled around him.

"I'm Willis Gingrich. Local blacksmith." He squatted beside her. "Can you tell me your name?"

The warmth and strength of his hand on her skin sent a sizzle of awareness along her nerve endings. "I'm Eva Coblentz. I am the new teacher and I'm fine now."

Don't miss
The Amish Teacher's Dilemma
by USA TODAY *bestselling author Patricia Davids,*
available March 2020 wherever
Love Inspired books and ebooks are sold.

LoveInspired.com